CONSTELLATION

by Adrien Bosc

TRANSLATED FROM THE FRENCH

by Willard Wood

INSTITUT
FRANÇAIS
ROYAUME-UNI
This book is supported by the Institut français (Royaume-Uni) as part of the Burgess programme

Supported using public funding by

**ARTS COUNCIL
ENGLAND**

This book has been selected to receive financial assistance from English PEN's PEN Translates! programme, supported by Arts Council England. English PEN exists to promote literature and our understanding of it, to uphold writers' freedoms around the world, to campaign against the persecution and imprisonment of writers for stating their views, and to promote the friendly co-operation of writers and the free exchange of ideas. *www.englishpen.org*

This paperback edition published in 2017

First published in Great Britain in 2016 by Serpent's Tail,
an imprint of Profile Books Ltd
3 Holford Yard
Bevin Way
London
WC1X 9HD
www.serpentstail.com

First published in French as *Constellation* by Editions Stock, Paris, 2014

Epigraph on page vii translated from the Italian by Tim Parks and published by Archipelago Books, New York, 2013

Copyright © Editions Stock 2014
Translation copyright © Willard Wood 2016

10 9 8 7 6 5 4 3 2 1

Designed by Julie Fry

Printed and bound by CPI Group (UK) Ltd, Croydon, CR0 4YY

A CIP record for this book can be obtained from the British Library

ISBN 978 1 78125 537 7
eISBN 978 1 78283 200 3

FSC
www.fsc.org
MIX
Paper from
responsible sources
FSC® C018072

ADRIEN BOSC was born in Avignon in 1986. He is the founder of Éditions du sous-sol and the magazines *Desports* and *Feuilleton*. *Constellation* is his first novel.

Praise for *Constellation*

"Stellar ... the stories of disparate people pulled together, like stars into orbit, by the force of one tragic moment. Like all great novels, *Constellation* works in ever expanding circles ... a meditation on chance, destiny, and the faults that lie sometimes in ourselves and sometimes in our stars" *Wall Street Journal*

"Slender yet ambitious ... echoing such classics as Thornton Wilder's *The Bridge of San Luis Rey* and Ernest K. Gann's *Fate Is the Hunter* ... a profound meditation on the far-reaching interconnectedness of tragic events" *Publishers Weekly*

"At once ambitious and accomplished in both narrative and prose style ... somewhere between novel, historical investigation and homage, *Constellation* sparkles ... Bosc goes about his investigation with great sensitivity ... finds signs, symmetries which illuminate and join the dots between these forty-eight stars snuffed out on 27 October 1949" *Le Figaro*

"Bosc adapts the story in a subtle and contemporary way to the thread of his obsessions ... an unsolvable investigation in which the fictional conflicts at every step with the real" *Liberation*

"Clear, chromed, spare ... Bosc has unearthed all the secrets, yet swirls around this steel tomb as if its enigma were inexhaustible. As if Lockheed Constellation F-BAZN were still charting its course to who knows where" *Nouvel Observateur*

526 192 82 6

for Laura

Sometimes the directions we take in our lives
can be decided by the combination of a few words.
— Antonio Tabucchi, *The Woman of Porto Pim*

Pierre Lazareff, editor of *France Soir*, the great French daily paper of the 1960s, once asked his friend Blaise Cendrars if he had really taken the Trans-Siberian Railway to write his *Prose of the Trans-Siberian*. The poet's answer came rocketing back, "What the hell does it matter, as long as I made you take it?" *Constellation* is unequivocally a novel, a truelife novel to probe the fiction at the heart of our lives, that ever more inventive, surprising, and unexpected reality. In its original and full meaning, the novel is "a fabulous work based on the most singular adventures in the life of man". (Sade, *Reflections on the Novel*)

Constellation

1 *Orly Airport*

I am the colossal drill
Boring into the startled husk of the night.
— Filippo Tommaso Marinetti, *The Pope's Monoplane*

On this night of October 27, 1949, on the tarmac at Orly, Air France's F-BAZN is waiting to receive thirty-seven passengers departing for the United States. A year earlier, Marcel Cerdan stepped off the plane as the newly crowned middleweight boxing champion of the world, a title he had wrested from Tony Zale. And on that October 7, 1948, the crowd lifted him on their shoulders in triumph. A year later, inside the airport with his manager, Jo Longman, and his friend Paul Genser, Cerdan is setting off to win back his title, now in the hands of Jake LaMotta, the Bronx Bull. There is no question that in December, on another Constellation, he will bring the title back with him. In the departure hall at Orly, he blusters to the journalists: "That title's coming home with me. I'm going to fight like a lion." Lion against Bull, a matter of signs and constellations. The Lion of Nemea vs. the Minotaur, mythical poster for December 2, 1949, at Madison Square Garden.

Jo Longman is wearing his bad-day face. They'd had to do everything in a hurry, cancel the passage on the ocean liner, claim priority seating on the Paris–New York flight, the whole can of worms, just to meet with Édith Piaf early the next morning. "Bring that title back with you!" says an Air France employee. "That's the whole idea of going!" says Marcel. "Ye-es," mutters Jo, who can't help adding, "If you'd listened to me, we'd have waited a few days. Jesus! We're sneaking off like thieves, almost. On Tuesday we learned the match was set for December 2, yesterday we were still out in the provinces, and today we barely had time to pack our bags. I said we should stay on for a week, attend the meet at the Palais des Sports. But no, that was too simple, and tomorrow you'll be rampaging around because, surprise surprise, in the rush to leave you'll have forgotten half your stuff." His anger is mock anger, they are used to playing at mutual recrimination, Marcel the amused free spirit and Jo the unheeded professional. In a few minutes, their elbows resting on the Air France bar, they'll laugh about it. Since the trainer Lucien Roupp quit, Jo has climbed in rank. Always in sunglasses, his hair pomaded, Jo Longman — who founded the Club des Cinq, the cabaret-restaurant where Édith and Marcel met — is the image of the louche character. The boxer likes his gift of the gab, his love of partying and head for business, finds him the perfect companion on long trips between Paris, New York, and Casablanca.

+

The "Aeroplane of the Stars" is living up to its name today. Besides the "Casablanca Clouter," the violin virtuoso Ginette Neveu is also setting off to conquer America. The tabloid *France-soir* organizes an impromptu photo session in the departure lounge. In the first snapshot, Jean Neveu stands in the centre smiling at his sister, while Marcel holds the Stradivarius and Ginette grins across at him. Next, Jo takes Jean Neveu's place and, with his expert's eye, compares the violinist's small hands with the boxer's powerful paws.

Then on the tarmac, at the foot of the gangway, the two celebrities continue their conversation. Ginette gives the details of her tour: Saint Louis, San Francisco, Los Angeles, Chicago, New York. Marcel offers her front-row seats for his rematch at Madison Square Garden and promises to attend the concert at Carnegie Hall on November 30. Maybe they can have dinner together at the Versailles, the cabaret where the Little Sparrow has been packing the house for months.

The four enormous Wright engines of Lockheed Constellation F-BAZN are droning. The propellers and blades have been inspected, and the eleven crew members line up in front of the plane. The big, beautiful aircraft, its aluminium fuselage perched on its outsized undercarriage, looks like a wading bird. In the boarding queue are thirty-two other passengers: John and Hanna Abbott, Mustapha Abdouni, Eghline Askhan, Joseph Aharony, Jean-Pierre Aduritz, Jean-Louis Arambel, Françoise and Jenny Brandière, Bernard Boutet de Monvel, Guillaume Chaurront, Thérèse Etchepare, Edouard Gehring, Remigio Hernandores, Simone Hennessy, René Hauth, Guy and Rachel Jasmin, Kay and Ketty Kamen, Emery Komios, Ernest Lowenstein, Amélie Ringler, Yaccob Raffo, Maud Ryan, Philip and Margarida Sales, Raoul Sibernagel, Irene Sivanich, Jean-Pierre Suquilbide, Edward Supine, and James Zebiner. Left behind are two newlyweds, Edith and Philip Newton, returning home from their honeymoon, and Mme Erdmann. The three were bumped when the champion received priority seating.

2 *A Dakota in Casablanca*

Modern life allows for travel but delivers no adventure.
—Jean Mermoz, *Mes vols* (My flights)

With bad weather reported over the Channel and the North
Atlantic, the pilot, Jean de la Noüe, decides to alter the
flight plan. In place of a stopover in Shannon, Ireland,
the plane will refuel on the small island of Santa Maria
in the Azores archipelago. The flight crew initiates the
departure sequence; head high, the big bird taxis from the
embarkation area towards the runway. The Curtiss propellers rumble in rhythm.

Pilot to control tower: "F-BAZN requests clearance for
takeoff."

Tower to pilot: "Clearance granted, F-BAZN."

At 20:06 hours, the Constellation takes flight.

Soon the Atlantic, in six hours the airfield at Santa Maria,
then Newfoundland, and tomorrow morning New York.

+

Almost six years after he joined the Free French Forces in London, Jean de La Noüe still thrills at the memory of his truant years flying rust buckets, at first British, then American.

He never could stomach the Phoney War and its aftermath. Still, he had taken his wife's advice and resumed work during the Occupation as a pilot for Air France, but the pill had grown progressively harder to swallow. He knew that it was all happening in London, and he wasn't there. In Pléneuf-Val-André, his village on the Brittany coast, the English cliffs in the distance, Free France and Radio London. To take service again over the Channel, the Atlantic, the Mediterranean, anywhere, as long as he was in the skies and on the right side. He had been only five years old when the armistice of the Great War was signed in a railway carriage in a forest clearing in Rethondes, and it was after discovering the exploits of the Dunkirk fighter squadron that he caught the aviation bug. His hero: Charles Nungesser, who disappeared over the Atlantic with François Coli while attempting a nonstop crossing in *L'Oiseau blanc* the year Jean turned fifteen. A pirate of the skies, Nungesser had painted his pilot's insignia on the fuselage of his two-seater, a Nieuport 17: a black heart encircling a skull and crossbones and a coffin set between two candles. Jean didn't have the makings of a hero, but he was no deserter. Demobilized in 1940, he had been sorry to exchange enemy lines for a commercial airline. In 1943, on his umpteenth flight,

Jean bolted and joined the Free French Forces. After the Allied landing in North Africa, he was assigned to transport soldiers from Casablanca to the Italian front. His aircraft was a Dakota, which the British pilots called the "Gooney Bird", or albatross, for its ungainliness on the ground and majesty in the skies.

+

Those flights over the Mediterranean were a long time ago, the best years of his life, he often said. The capture of Pantelleria Island on June 10, 1943, then Linosa, Lampedusa, and the celebrated invasion of Sicily. Thirty-eight days of ferrying forces from the advanced base on Pantelleria, twenty-eight men to a Dakota. And leaving in his wake, as he shuttled back and forth, traceries of parachute canopies in the sky. Operation Avalanche on Salerno, and Slapstick to take the port of Taranto. The great battle, Monte Cassino, would come on May 11, 1944. Then parachute drops over Provence. In Casablanca, the Allied rear base, Jean would return to life. History was in the making, and he was part of it, an extra in the great theatre of operations organized by Churchill and Roosevelt at the Casablanca Conference. De Gaulle, Giraud, a few demobilized veterans from the French Naval Air Force, and the French Army, which was now the second blade of the Allied operation — all these men, tenacious and battle-hardened, hungered for revenge and reconquest. In the postwar years, he brought his wife to the Max Linder cinema to see *Casablanca* with Ingrid Bergman and Humphrey Bogart. He took exception to the casbah, so much at variance with his own recollections, and laughed out loud at the singing of the *Marseillaise* led by the resistance fighter Laszlo. Total joke. Walking back up the boulevard Poissonnière, he described his Casablanca to Aurore. The hotel in the Anfa district and the restaurant with the panoramic view. The palm groves around Camp Cazes airfield and the barracks where the pilots were packed together. The runway, which features as the final set of the film, where Rick Blaine and Captain Renault celebrate the beginning of a beautiful friendship. He told her too about the history of the Moroccan airmail service, about the exploits of Mermoz and Saint-Exupéry, flying over the desert, over sand dunes, where you see nothing, hear nothing, and beauty is hidden in immensity.

On the night of October 27, 1949, Jean de La Noüe, captain aboard F-BAZN, has sixty thousand flight hours and eighty-eight transatlantic crossings to his credit. Next to him are Charles Wolfer and Camille Fidency, two former combat pilots. Since hostilities ended there has been no front to receive these soldiers. Like Jean, they chose not to pursue a career in naval aviation, adapting instead to this new line of commercial work. Assigned to the same flights, the two have become friends. And born the same hour on December 4, 1920, they are known in the company as the "astrological twins". Soon, between stopovers, they will celebrate their twenty-ninth birthday. The radio is manned by Roger Pierre and Paul Giraud, the navigator is Jean Salvatori. And André Villet and Marcel Sarrazin, mechanics, complete the flight crew.

3 The Signal is Erratic

The aeroplane! The aeroplane! May it climb to the sky,
Soar over the peaks, and cross the watery divide.
— Guillaume Apollinaire, "L'Avion" in *Poèmes retrouvés*
   (Rediscovered poems)

"The new comet from Air France," read the advertising brochures. The Constellation was going to supplant luxury ocean liners and establish the dominance of air over sea. A chrome-plated bird born of the folly of one man, Howard Hughes.

The majority shareholder of Trans World Airlines, Hughes had launched the project to build the "Connie" in 1939. Working with Lockheed Aircraft, the film and aviation magnate proposed a new gamble: a pressurized four-engine passenger plane capable of travelling 3,500 miles in one hop. He drew the plans freehand, his sketches guided by a taste for elegance and eroticism, leaving to the engineers the task of adapting them to the laws of aeronautics.

During that same period, for the shooting of *The Outlaw*, Hughes designed a cantilevered bra with steel undercup rods that turned Jane Russell's breasts into missiles aimed at the screen and at the leagues of public decency.

Initially brought into the U.S. Army Air Force programme and used for troop transport between continents, the Constellation logged its first commercial flight in 1944 when, with its eccentric billionaire at the controls, it shattered existing records by flying from Burbank, California, to Washington, D.C., in six hours and fifty-seven minutes. On February 15, 1946, the producer–aviator invited a group of Hollywood luminaries on a nonstop flight from New York to Los Angeles. At an altitude of twenty-five thousand feet, flanked by Paulette Goddard and Linda Darnell, and holding a megaphone in one hand and a glass of champagne in the other, Hughes presented his new toy. With the Constellation and its stars, aviation was entering an era of aluminized luxury. But though it was a symbol of the prop-driven transatlantic airliner at its zenith, the Connie's early flights belied its eventual destiny. Singular law of series. On June 18, 1946, one of the four engines of a Pan Am Constellation caught fire. The pilot managed to remain in the air over the continental United States for eleven hours all the same. The Constellation, which the press dubbed "the best three-engine aircraft in the world", suffered another accident twenty-three days later when a Connie made an emergency landing in a field, killing five of its six passengers. As a precaution, all Constellations were grounded until Lockheed could effect the necessary changes. Once the adjustments were made, a few months later, the Constellation again received its certificate of airworthiness and established itself as the premier long-range aircraft for transport companies worldwide. Among them was Air France, once privately held but now nationalized, which ordered thirteen planes from Lockheed. The first Air France Constellation, registration number F-BAZA, took off from La Guardia Airport on July 9, 1946, Roger Loubry its captain. Starting on October 8, 1947, when Air France inaugurated its "Golden Comet" luxury service, the carrier could boast of being the only airliner to offer sleeping berths on transatlantic routes, reducing the sixteen-hour flight to a long night's sleep.

Once the French coastline is behind them, the stewardess, Suzanne Roig, and the two stewards, Albert Brucker and Raymond Redon, busy themselves around the cabin. Marcel Cerdan, after a brief courtesy visit to the cockpit, sits next to his friend Paul Genser. In front of them is Jo Longman, in conversation with the journalist René Hauth, editor in chief of an Alsace daily newspaper. The latter is asking about the champion's physical condition, his regimen, the training camp they have chosen, and any concerns the manager might have, for a dispatch he'll telegraph to his editors from New York in the morning. A golden opportunity to gather firsthand information in mid-flight. Air travel's happy coincidences bring about the most improbable encounters. In the back of the plane, Jean and Ginette Neveu talk in undertones and meet their neighbour, Edward Supine, a lace importer from Brooklyn returning from a business trip to Calais. Somewhat embarrassed, he admits to not knowing much about music but promises to listen to one of their recordings and asks the virtuoso to spell her name. Guy Jasmin, four seats back, starts reading *Moby-Dick*, which he bought the previous day at the Gallimard bookstore on the boulevard Raspail. The opening words are unmistakably engaging: *"Je m'appelle Ishmaël. Mettons."* "Call me Ishmael. Some years ago — never mind how long precisely — having little or no money in my purse, and nothing in particular to interest me on the shore, I thought I would sail about a little and see the watery part of the world."

To his right, Ernest Lowenstein, who owns tanneries in France and Morocco, is still marvelling at being on the same flight as Marcel Cerdan. He manages to approach the champion and get his autograph in a notebook. The stewardess, wearing a pleated skirt, a navy-blue jacket, and a beret with the airline's sea horse insignia, patrols the central aisle — on one side is a row of reclining seats and on the other curtained sleeping alcoves — passing out meal trays to the passengers: beef in aspic, lamb stew, and macarons, accompanied by champagne. Air France has been offering hot meals on its planes since September 30, a first for many of the passengers. The idea came from Max Hymans, the company's president, who created the catering service at

Orly a few months earlier, enlisting several great Parisian chefs for the venture.

Thirteen thousand nine hundred feet above the Atlantic, the Constellation transmits its position to Orly at 21:00 hours and proceeds on a diagonal toward the Azores. The plane, travelling at 250 miles per hour, will reach the Santa Maria airport at 2:30 in the morning GMT. Its cruising speed attained, the aircraft seems to be soaring. In the pilot's cabin, Jean de La Noüe lets go of the control column and puts his two copilots in charge. Communicating directly with Air France's operation centre, Roger Pierre reads out the weather report.

"Captain, Paris has just confirmed the flight plan radioed to Santa Maria. A low-pressure system is expected over the islands at arrival time, with limited visibility on the ground."

+

It is almost 23:00 hours when Jean de La Noüe resumes control of the aircraft while passing through a zone of turbulence. He decides to climb and settle the plane above the cloud cover. In the cabin, the passengers are falling asleep, rocked by the rhythmic drone of the propellers. A few minutes before the descent, the captain will wake them up to fasten their seat belts and prepare for landing. A first three-hour nap, before the long northward leg to Newfoundland.

Jean is not an affable man, his style of command is marked by silence — a few well-chosen words, nothing flowery — only what it takes to keep the flight on track. A taciturn authority. He rarely talks about the war and his exploits, unlike his two copilots, whose first exposure to flight was in the naval air force. Veteran pilots bored with the monotonous southern route to the Americas, they are arguing the merits of the latest fighter planes and describing the performance characteristics of the Soviet MiG-9 and Yak-15, compared with the U.S. Air Force's F-84 Thunderjet. And touting the efforts of French aviation, which, after a late start, produced the SO.6000 Triton, a single-engine two-seater with a maximum speed of 592 miles per hour — about 200 miles below the sound barrier broken by Chuck Yeager in the Bell X-1, the experimental plane shaped like a sparrow hawk. The French airmail service had pushed the envelope by "always giving it a try" and "always taking off", but now there were new limits, sonic and spatial.

At one in the morning, from 185 miles away, the plane makes contact with the Santa Maria control tower. In the first exchanges, the Constellation is instructed to regulate its transmitter. The signal, according to airport authorities, is erratic, the tuning off. Radio beacon guidance along the Azores line confirms the aircraft's ideal position. The regional centre announces optimal weather conditions and good visibility at ground level.

4 The Monvel Folly

Their town, unbelievably, stood straight up.

—Louis-Ferdinand Céline, *Journey to the End of the Night*

Bernard Boutet de Monvel disliked air travel. This was not a phobia. He had been a pilot. A hero, in fact. Called up in 1914, he distinguished himself in exploits over the Bay of the Somme, then on a brilliant raid from Salonika to Bucharest. Despite this, he much preferred the leisurely pace of transatlantic ocean liners, flying only when necessary. A man from an earlier century, the representative of a world in decline, one soon to be surpassed by the reign of hurried men, Boutet de Monvel would concur with Paul Valéry in his *Outlook for Intelligence:* "Duration has become unendurable. We have lost the art of fecundating boredom." As a painter of uninflected lines, of plane geometry, he enjoyed looking at the rectilinear perfection of luxury liners. The soft underbelly of the twentieth century, which he was traversing despite himself, seemed far more the end of an era than the interwar years ever had. He felt the race had passed him by, and he happily relaxed his pace. In response to the new man, he offered a caricature of another time. His dandyism, which he pushed to the limit, his impeccable dress, his pronounced good manners, all served to counter the general haste. A slight step to the side in his patent leather ankle boots, a source of secret delight, jumping the rails in his three-piece suit away from the world's ongoing march. Those anonymous crowds lost among tall buildings, vast train stations, giant streets had obsessed him once. The setting struck him as the perfect transcription of an ideal, a contest between flat shapes, massiveness framed in a vertical design. The avant-garde's dismissal of him was more reassuring than painful, he saw it as a form of recognition. His being out of step, raised to an ethic, had set him swimming irremediably against the tide. Thus it was in 1926, with the Paris art world at the height of its influence, that he immigrated to the United States, only to return to Paris briefly in the middle of World War II, when New York became the chosen place of exile for European artists. A hopscotching course that sometimes worked to his disadvantage. Having vowed to shake off the label of society painter, he unintentionally became, on the far side of the Atlantic, the portraitist to the millionaires, the leading painter of café society. He had painted landscapes of Fez after the Great War, made sketches for *Harper's Bazaar* aboard ocean liners, drawn steel mills in Chicago and views of Grand Central Terminal, but what brought him fame and adulation were his full-length portraits. Already in 1908, it was his self-portrait, an act of artistic masochism, that had earned him the recognition of his peers at the French Society of Fine Arts. At the society's exhibition, amused, he'd responded to the presentation of his work with a falsely modest quip: "No, nothing to speak of, a portrait of myself." When you try to undermine yourself, sometimes you succeed. A paradoxical position suggesting that failure may have its good sides. Thus when the stock market crashed in 1929, he celebrated. As millionaires jumped from skyscrapers, his commissions became scarcer, and he was able to concentrate on painting the empty expanses of the New World. A fecund depression, no longer painting the tired flesh of proud souls but concrete vistas instead. The factory and not its boss, the high-rise in place of its owner.

With his aristocratic face marked by deep blue eyes and clear features, ennobled by a broad forehead, Boutet de Monvel — his hair slicked, his dress invariably fastidious — had a cold, implacable, commanding beauty. He hardly ever disturbed this royal engraving. Monvel was a quiet eccentric, nothing advertised the madcap spark within him. A night owl of the early century, he had been a regular at Maxim's. Night after night, he and his gang rivalled one another at cheating boredom. Still today he remembers with hilarity his sidekick, Ravaud, dressing as an omnibus driver and taking his passengers out to the village of Pontoise. Monvel was stone-faced, impeccable, drawing enjoyment from every situation, even the most alarming. In the middle of World War II, he gathered all the members of his family to pose in front of his country house in gas masks, and the surrealistic snapshot was prominently displayed in his New York apartment.

His eccentricity was engraved in the stone of a hexagonal villa built in Palm Beach in 1936 and unironically christened "La Folie Monvel", the Monvel Folly.

On this night of October 27, Monvel is bringing his periodic exiles to a close. Now almost seventy years old, he has vowed never to set foot in the United States after this trip. He has sold the Folie Monvel, packed up his other life in trunks and shipped it home, and the painter is looking forward to his retirement in France. A few months earlier, a project had amused him for a while. In February 1948, he received a strange call from RKO Pictures asking if he would drop everything and paint a portrait of Ingrid Bergman for the release of *Joan of Arc*. For several days, in a suite at the Hampshire House hotel in New York City, the star had posed for him holding a sword. Her admirer since seeing Hitchcock's *Notorious*, he secretly took pleasure in thumbing his nose at his family history. His father, Maurice Boutet de Monvel, an illustrator of the late nineteenth century, was famous for his *Jeanne d'Arc*, an album of historical sketches with watercolour illustrations reproduced in zinc plate. The circle closes, he told himself. An unwitting gift from RKO Pictures.

In the autumn of 1949, the papers were singing the praises of Victor Fleming, *Joan of Arc*'s director. André Bazin called the film "faithful and moving". But Monvel had not had time to attend a screening, he was finishing a commission for the socialite Mary Rogers, which was due at the end of October. The fact that the painter was among the passengers of F-BAZN was the result of a strange series of events. Politeness, that organized indifference, was playing one last trick on him. Monvel had been scheduled to take his final trip with the actress Françoise Rosay aboard the flight leaving Wednesday, October 26. During boarding, the actress had so much excess luggage that Monvel graciously offered his seat to her. Happy to make the gesture, he assured her that a day's delay would in no way affect his schedule, that any failure on his part to help would upset him far more than missing the plane. Making elegant use of a *bon mot*, he added, "Remember Bergson, who said that the spirit of politeness is no more than a kind of flexibility. And this evening, dear Françoise, you are giving my empirical mind a chance to prove it."

5 "I Have the Field in Sight!"

Aeroplanes weave the telegraph lines.
—Philippe Soupault, *"Dimanche"* (Sunday)

In the aeroplane, the cabin crew are preparing to wake the passengers in the sleeping berths. It is two in the morning, and the flight plan calls for Air France's F-BAZN to land in forty-five minutes on the tarmac at Santa Maria for refuelling. Other than a little chop, the flight has been peaceful, uneventful. Roger Pierre radios the airport with the estimated time of arrival: 2:45 a.m. A few minutes later, the Portuguese control tower confirms clearance to land. At the controls, Jean de La Noüe pushes the stick forward, then stabilizes the craft at 8,800 feet above sea level. It is only the third time the pilot has landed in the Azores. He normally flies the northern route and touches down in Ireland, where the crew make full use of the duty-free shops, having nicknamed Shannon "Whiskey Airport."

Santa Maria is one of nine islands in the Azores, volcanic outcrops in the middle of the ocean. Its airport looks like a rural runway, the landing strip on an aeroplane carrier. Windswept, the archipelago has always been a port of call, whether for oceangoing or airborne craft. The last step before the big leap. The outbound point of departure and the point of return on coming back.

Thirty minutes before arrival, F-BAZN radios the control tower to signal a ten-minute delay in the agreed schedule and to request permission to continue its slow descent to 5,000 feet. Permission is granted, and the tower describes the weather on the ground, clear skies and perfect visibility. In the cockpit, Jean de La Noüe and his two copilots, focused and confident, proceed with final manoeuvres, all the more reassured by the weather conditions on the island. At 2:50 a.m., F-BAZN confirms its arrival time. In five minutes the plane will touch down at Santa Maria. After receiving its final clearance, as per protocol, the plane approaches at 3,300 feet. Landing particulars are relayed to the Constellation, wind speed and direction, as well as the runway number. The pilot acknowledges: "Roger." The radio alphabet captures the imagination, as do the esoteric utterances of marine weather radio: Dogger, Fisher, hectopascal, freshening southwest, Viking, Beaufort scale, tidal bore, the celebrated Azores High. And the response, in encrypted language: Alpha, Bravo, Charlie, Delta, Echo, Foxtrot, Golf, Hotel, India, Juliette, Kilo, Lima, Mike, November, Oscar, Papa, Quebec, Romeo, Sierra, Tango,

Uniform, Victor, Whiskey, X-ray, Yankee, Zulu. Technology and its language, those formulas produced with a magic wand. Context aside, the difference between advanced technology and magic is negligible, the point being simply to levitate an airframe of several tons.

The passengers are strapped in, Marcel Cerdan jokes with Jo Longman, while Paul Genser stares fixedly out of the porthole. Ginette Neveu clasps the case containing her two violins, a Stradivarius and a Guadagnini—a week ago she owned only one. At the front of the aeroplane, their seat harnesses cinched, the cockpit crew prepare for landing.

Seeing land ahead, Jean de La Noüe announces, "I have the field in sight!" The approach to the field is shrouded in thick fog, lights pierce the celestial haze, and the crew is puzzled at the rain and greyish cotton wool enveloping the cabin. Didn't they say the airport had perfect visibility? The three pilots are perplexed. It must be some uncorrected error in translation. At the navigation table, Roger Pierre and Jean Salvatori check the coordinates transmitted by the ground beacons. Above the monitor, a metal panel screwed into the plastic sidewall reads EMERGENCY EXIT. The runway lights ahead, dimmed by the clouds, signal the approaching airport. The hatches open, the wheel assemblies emerge from the belly of F-BAZN, and the plane drops towards the Santa Maria airfield.

At 2:51:02 a.m. a last message from the tower to the Constellation hangs unanswered.

6 The Age of Nylon

Under their dress, you'll find panties, a bra,
and, for vanity, a nylon slip.
— Elsa Triolet, *The Age of Nylon*

A vast confluence of causes determines the most unlikely
result. Forty-eight people, forty-eight agents of uncertainty enfolded within a series of innumerable reasons,
fate is always a question of perspective. A modelized aeroplane in which forty-eight story fragments form a world.
An impromptu survey whose description goes beyond the
very conformity of studies. A census of men, of women. A
standard cross-sectional sample, as Charlotte Delbo wrote
in *Le Convoi du 24 janvier*, the account of her convoy to Aus-
chwitz — 230 women, 230 civil records, rows of facts, dates,
places, which, by the plain power of their arrangement and
sequence, are freed from the straitjacket of form. Lives,
tiny and huge, matryoshka dolls. Six years earlier, Amélie
Ringler could have been one of those women. She could

have put a pile of tracts about the Resistance into her shoulder bag, become a political prisoner, been herded into the transit camp at Romainville, into the convoy, the extermination camp. Amélie would have been twenty-one years old. The city of Mulhouse was no longer Mulhouse but Mülhausen, in territory annexed by the Third Reich. Eighteen years old when Hitler and his retinue paraded through the streets. From the Schlucht Pass, the straight-armed procession of the Wehrmacht had wound its way into the old city. Within a few days, all the streets had German names. The rue du Sauvage (Street of the Savage) had become Adolf-Hitler-Strasse, a perfect translation that remained in place only long enough to spark general hilarity. The name was quickly changed to the more literal Wildemannstrasse. Twenty-two years old when, on the morning of November 21, 1944, she watched in astonishment as the Senegalese 6th Rifle Brigade and French troops entered the city under the command of General Lattre de Tassigny. Two days of fighting until, on November 23, the Moroccan 7th Rifle Company and a supporting tank unit captured the Lefèbre Barracks, the last German strongpoint.

Amélie is flying on the Constellation towards a destiny she hardly could have hoped for, an extraordinary opportunity, truly incredible, which she had greeted with total disbelief a few weeks earlier. A spool operator in a textile mill in Mulhouse, Amélie is the eldest of ten children. "Amélie"

is also the name of the potassium mine where her father works. North of Mulhouse lies a series of shafts named after Protestant heirs: Eugène, Alex, Joseph-Else, Fernand, Théodore, Max, Rodolphe. Her family lives in the workers' village that the Mulhouse Industrial Society built near the mine works. Every morning, her brothers join her father in the potassium mines, while Amélie and her sisters work at the Dollfus-Mieg & Co. cotton mill—makers of the DMC yarns whose brand is posted on the storefronts of notions shops. The Ringler sisters are spoolers in the production of mouliné, a yarn whose cotton threads can be separated indefinitely. Spools, balls of yarn, skeins, carded and combed, put up in hanks, destined to be threaded through the eye of an embroidery needle. At Amélie's cradle, no hidden fairy was present to foretell that the child would prick her finger on a spindle, yet her incredible story does include a godmother who watches over her fate. Amélie was in her twenty-seventh year when a letter of prophecy arrived. Her godmother had left Alsace for the United States in the 1930s. People knew she was rich, but no one imagined just how rich she was. She'd started as a worker in Detroit and become the director of a large factory for nylon stockings. A spinster and childless, she had focused all her energies on her career, and with her fortune now made, she was calling her goddaughter to her side. The whole family gathered on a September evening to read the letter from the almost forgotten aunt. Its message was not in doubt: Amélie was to be her sole heir. In the envelope was a money order for two hundred thousand francs to cover the cost of the trip.

Everything happened so quickly, and, at Orly on October 27, Amélie is still trying to take it all in. She wants the news confirmed firsthand; the prophecy still hangs in the air. It is her first trip, and she is sixteen thousand feet above an ocean she has never seen. The day before, in transit, she took advantage of some idle hours to wander through the Bon Marché department store. She bought a long green dress, a scarf, and a pair of nylon stockings from Schiaparelli. Amélie has long, dark hair, tied back under a black straw hat, her short fringe peeping out. Green, almond-shaped eyes. She wears a silver necklace with an Egyptian medallion, an ankh amulet, symbol of eternal life. Once inside Air France's F-BAZN, she sits next to another young woman, Françoise Brandière. They are about the same age, could almost be sisters. While Amélie will catch a train to Detroit tomorrow at Grand Central Terminal, Françoise will board a second flight to Cuba.

Ten years later, Elsa Triolet would embark on her *Age of Nylon* trilogy—*Roses à crédit*, *Luna-Park*, and *L'Âme*—sketching a period still in the process of defining itself, a moment when people's outlooks, tastes, and dreams were evolving. Amélie could have been one of the heroines of that narrative, a leading one. The cotton-mill worker, a future queen of nylon production, the spooler from Old Europe who becomes an industrialist in the New World. The passage from the age of silk to the age of nylon, from a living to a synthetic fabric.

7 Off the Azores

...1027 millibars near the Azores, with a ridge of
1025 millibars extending towards Spain.

—Marie-Pierre Planchon, *Météo marine* (Marine forecast)

Several minutes have passed since ground control last radioed the Lockheed Constellation. Palpable anxiety, the plane
should already be taxiing on runway number one at Santa
Maria airfield. No sound, no light or explosion troubles the
island's clear sky. F-BAZN has vanished into thin air. The
two controllers on duty in the tower send out another call
in vain. The line stays silent. At 2:53 a.m. the alarm is raised.
The searchers focus first on the expanse of sea around the
Azores. The Constellation has foundered at sea, no other
explanation is likely. "To founder at sea", those maritime
words, expressions, verbs...

To founder at sea, ply the seas, jump into the sea, take
to the sea, go to sea, die at sea, toss a bottle into the sea, be
drowned, swamped, lost at sea, carried off to sea, to harrow,

scour, sail the Seven Seas, disappear at sea, crisscross the southern seas, drive towards, end up with one's back against the sea, at the bottom of the sea, old salt, sea wolf, fortune of the sea, a high, a full, a low, a heavy sea, that retreats, lays bare, rises, roars, forms whitecaps, bites into, wears at, undermines, erodes the cliffs, washes the shore, sparkles, glitters, glows, subsides, goes glassy, retreats, foams, unfurls, crests and falls, an oily sea, a sea of ice, of sand, a secondary sea, a bordering sea, an inland sea, landlocked, cold, temperate, frozen, calm, angry, swollen, stormy, flat, tropical, Arthur Rimbaud's star-studded and lactescent sea, the furious lapping of the tides, the sidereal archipelagos and the islands whose delirious skies are opened to the seafarer: Is it on these bottomless nights that the aeroplane falls asleep and enters exile?

The island's rescue craft set forth on the ocean in search of the wreck and its survivors, as they hope, or its casualties, as they fear. Searchlights bolted to their bows, sweeping the reefs and the Atlantic as far as their beams can reach. A black night, the wail of the siren, the coming and going of the lights, and the steadfast fear, mounting as the minutes pass inexorably. One-thirty a.m. on the archipelago. The dawn that will reveal the sea's vast tracts is still some distance off. There's no trace of an aeroplane around the patrol boats furrowing the reefs and distant waters, no fuselage, no wreckage, no cry of distress shatters the silence; only the restless sea, the sound of motors, of waves being pounded, of water lapping against hulls. A resonant silence.

The silence you hear when, perhaps no more than once, you make a night crossing, a deafening silence, massive, a sky that is empty and filled with stars, a paradox.

In his *Almagest*, a summation of mathematical and astronomical knowledge, Ptolemy offered the first analytical map of the celestial vault, identifying 1,022 stars and forty-eight constellations. In the Azores, after dusk, in an aeroplane named for a grouping of stars, forty-eight people go missing. At 2:00 a.m., 3:00 a.m., 4:00 a.m., 5:00 a.m., no sign awakens the Atlantic. Reflected in the infinite puddle are the Great and Little Bears, Orion, and Scorpio.

8 *Five Basque Shepherds*

"Hey, we're here, us shepherds!"
—Jean Giono, *Le serpent d'étoiles* (*The Serpent of Stars*)

On Wednesday, October 26, 1949, five Basque shepherds stand on the platform of the Bordeaux-Saint-Jean train station. Their dream is to return home having made their fortunes. Four boys, one girl, all from farming families.

Thérèse Etchepare is a child of twenty with dark, almond-shaped eyes. She clutches her canvas bag to keep from crying. She will work as a domestic servant at a ranch in Tempe, Arizona. Three thousand animals, veal calves, cows, hogs. She'll stay there for ten years. Then she'll come home with her savings. She made the decision two months ago and, on Tuesday, dragged herself away from her family.

The oldest of the five shepherds, Guillaume Chaurront, is a handsome young man of twenty-eight. He feels no regret at leaving his village and has always dreamed of the wide-open plains, over there, in California.

Jean-Louis Arambel, nineteen, is the youngest of the group from Aldudes. He leaves behind his parents and three brothers. It will mean one less mouth to feed, and he is hoping for a better future. There won't be tears at his departure. He plans to live with his uncle, a farmer in Los Banos, California. His sweetheart, Maritchu, to whom he gave a long kiss the night before he left, will surely wait ten years for him. They have sworn a solemn promise to each other and sealed their pact on the crest of a hill. When he comes home, they will buy a piece of land together, down below, in the valley.

Jean-Pierre Aduritz has less to lose and little to gain. But he's going. At twenty-one, he has been a domestic servant in Aldudes since the age of five. The shepherd's contract he has in his pocket is enough to make him happy. His four sisters can maybe join him over there someday. At least he hopes so.

Jean-Pierre Suquilbide, twenty-five, a servant like Aduritz, is the eldest of seven children. He is not particularly ambitious, but he is glad to be going to Pocatello, Idaho. He wants one day, in ten years maybe, to buy a white house in his village. He has met them in the shade of the pelota courts, the elders who returned from America, and has heard their stories of horses, of cowboys, of vast grasslands in Wyoming, Texas, Colorado. They even spoke some *English* for amusement.

The five young shepherds are emigrating so as to come back, leaving so as to settle later in the valley, a huge detour, the only solution open to them. Their hope is to find the cousins, brothers, friends who went before, the famous shepherds who exchanged trails through the Pyrenees for other, unknown mountains on a ranchman's contract of ten, fifteen years, after which they returned home, wealthy and proud, to become, in the villagers' eyes, "the Americans".

Basque shepherds had earned a good reputation, were known for their love of work and animals. Landless shepherds in their own country, they found tracts of land on the boundless frontier to clear and cultivate. The vast distances were new to them, the seasonal migration stretched over several months — winter in the desert, spring at an altitude of almost ten thousand feet. The salary was $170 a month, and the currency was strong, with the exchange rate at 350 francs to the dollar. Hundreds of shepherds and farmers from the Basque country immigrated to the United States in the decades from the 1930s to the 1960s, forming a Basque diaspora. They retained their language from across the Atlantic, a unified community, improvising matches of pelota in the barns of the New World. Some never returned, some married there, some died in the United States. *Ohore zuri euskal artzaina*, "All honour to you, Basque shepherd", would read the epitaph, or else these verses by Grégoire Iturria:

> *Tranpa gorria*
> *Hunarat etorria*
> *Untsa urrikitia*
> *Fitesko hustu behar tokia.*

Coming here
Is a trap
A regret
A place soon to be left behind.

On the train, the five shepherds, escorted by M. Monlong, talk loudly back and forth. The three Jeans from Aldudes — Jean-Louis Arambel, Jean-Pierre Aduritz, and Jean-Pierre Suquilbride — joke with one another as distant relatives do. The three villagers soon find that they share a cousin with Guillaume Chaurront and Thérèse Etchepare. In the valley, everyone is family. The shepherds' compartment in the second-class carriage echoes with the local dialect of the Quint region, on the border of Navarre and Lower Navarre, featured by Prince Louis-Lucien Bonaparte in his *Map of the Seven Basque Provinces*, published in 1863. They sing airs from the home country, with Jean-Louis offering a chorus of "All summer long, the nesting quail sings his sweet song." The sadness of departure, the nostalgia for their home valley, is displaced by the foretaste of the great adventure ahead, of the internal boundaries dropping away as they advance. Behind them are the 920 residents who stayed, the pelota courts, the white houses with brown doors and shutters, the landscape divided by the Nourèpe, the village's river. They talk about the aeroplane, about flying, how crazy it is.

At the Gare d'Austerlitz, the five youngsters and their chaperone discover Paris for the first time. From their base at the Hôtel du Terminus, they pore over a map of the city and identify the key spots to visit. On Thursday, October 27, at the top of the Eiffel Tower, M. Monlong immortalizes their voyage. The group photo shows, from left to right, the two Jean-Pierres, Guillaume, and Jean-Louis; and seated in the middle, a short, dark-haired girl stares into the lens, Thérèse. Across the top of the snapshot, a pen scrawl in the sky over Paris gives the place and date.

The shepherds cling together inside Orly Airport and reconvene at the back of the aeroplane, picking up the conversation that has been going nonstop since they left the train station in Bordeaux. At first excited, they grow apprehensive about the flight, then as the plane tucks itself between two clouds, the conversation flows again. Cerdan is just a dozen yards away. They can't get over it.

9 *Scrolls*

Dawns are heartbreaking.
— Arthur Rimbaud, "The Drunken Boat"

Dawn is breaking over the Azores archipelago. Boats belonging to the Portuguese authorities are still hoping to find traces of the Constellation. Eight aeroplanes take off from the Santa Maria airfield looking for F-BAZN. They fly over the island, the mountainous ridge of the Serra Verde, the Pico Alto, scrutinize in length and breadth this rock thrust upward by the sole force of a volcano. Santa Maria is an oceanic island, a few thousand herders and fishermen are isolated on this steamboat stalled in the middle of the Atlantic. This morning, Friday, October 28, 1949, the aeroplanes trace the outlines of a boundary scrawled with the diagonals of contrails. White cross-hatching, like a map of the archipelago.

Several hours elapse, the Constellation remains unfound, vaporized in a triangle of the Azores. Paulo

Gomes's search plane strays from the area targeted by the authorities and explores to the north, farther out, towards the islands of São Miguel and Terceira. A hunch. Halfway between Santa Maria and São Miguel, the pilot sees, rising from Mount Redondo like an Indian signal, a smoke cloud, a coiling scroll of smoke that adds several yards to the mountain. Above its belt of haze, the telegraphic puffs sing:

> *Scrolls of coiling smoke*
> *Your toils gone*
> *Clouds broken open*

Paulo Gomes continues north and flies over Mount Redondo at an altitude of four thousand feet, circling the summit, and discovers the dislocated carcass of the Constellation smouldering on the mountainside. The ripped-off wings and, a few hundred yards below, the remainder of the four-engine plane. A pool in the centre burns with the last litres of kerosene from the aircraft. Around the dismembered wading bird are figures in motion, seemingly survivors.

> *Scrolls of coiling smoke*
> *Drift past the dimmed eyes*
> *Of flashing dragonflies*

Hope rises again in the search plane, and the pilot sends the information to the control centre. A few minutes later, the authorities on Santa Maria send a telegram to Lisbon: F-BAZN AIRCRAFT FOUND ALGARVIA PEAK LOCATED NORTHWEST SAO MIGUEL STOP PLANE SAYS THERE ARE SURVIVORS STOP GOING CLOSER TO LOOK STOP. The message was intercepted by Air France in Paris during the early afternoon. As boats from the island made their way to São Miguel, the airline sent its own rescue mission by plane.

Scrolls of coiling smoke
Drift in plumes
Toward enchanted flutes
While cruel hopes pierce
With daggers and darts
An innocent heart

A succession of events, interconnected,
that would cancel each other out.
— Georges Perec, *Life, a User's Manual*

One tragedy can hide another. When Jenny Brandière
returned to France in June 1949, it was to rush to the bed-
side of her daughter Françoise. During the early summer
in Havana, there had been nothing to suggest the tragic
events unfolding in Paris. Françoise was studying for her
degree in Spanish at the Language Institute and had been
living for the past year in the family apartment on the boulevard Malesherbes in the 17th Arrondissement, not far from
the avenue de Wagram and the parish of Saint Francis de
Sales. It was the summer she turned twenty-one. Coming
back from a party that her cousins gave outside Paris, the
Citroën Traction Avant 11 CV driven by her friend Gérard
slammed full tilt into a roadside tree. On the far side of
the shattered windshield, the mangled bonnet, the chevron

insignia bent back to the wheels, smoke pouring out against the wounded trunk, the two passengers thrown from the car. Françoise was taken to the hospital in critical condition, comatose from cranial trauma. Her older sister, Monique, her aunt, Denise, attended her between life and death. It was generally believed that she had no chance. A string of emergency surgeries was performed. Both legs were shattered. In the hallway, sitting on a stool, his features drawn, was a family friend, the conductor Charles Munch.

Notified immediately, Jenny Brandière took the next flight from Havana to Paris, pausing in New York. The prognosis was still uncertain when she arrived. Watching her daughter's unconscious form, Jenny vowed to bring her back to Cuba. A few days later, Professeur Puech called for a trepanation, and once the hematoma was evacuated the patient came out of her coma. The operation had been a success, she returned gradually to life. Transferred to the Diaconesses Clinic, she underwent a long and painful convalescence, her visiting hours growing progressively longer, the fragments of words becoming sentences, discussions, questions, answers. She would always limp. In August, she took her first walks at their country house in the Yonne. She asked to return to the site of the accident, a snapshot showed her at the foot of the tree wearing the smile of a survivor, carrying a cane, treading on the grass at the edge of the country road. In September, she returned to the apartment on the boulevard Malesherbes. They decided not to enrol her at the university for the year ahead. She would leave for Cuba in early November. On the far side of the world, a husband and father, Jean Brandière, ill, moved up the departure date. It would be October 27.

In 1899, with six hundred dollars in his pocket, Albert Brandière disembarked in what was still only a Spanish colony and created an import–export business in Cuba for French goods. In his suitcase, between two shirts, suspenders, and socks, were the flagship products of the Guerlain and Vichy brands, a leather shop-front for an industry he hoped to import. Through good years and bad, the business grew, gradually narrowing its activities to represent French pharmaceutical products. Brandière Laboratories packaged the raw material and made a line of medicines from Old Europe available in Havana. In 1927, Albert's eldest son, Jean, was chosen to lead the business. September 1939, the sound of boots was echoing from continent to continent, the Brandières were returning to France aboard a ship flying the American flag. A reserve officer in the French Army, Jean was imprisoned. Two years in Oflag XIII, now a father of four, he was released. Back in Paris, weakened by renal tuberculosis, not forgetting his companions in misfortune who remained in Germany, he joined the Red Cross, working actively for their repatriation. The German surrender prompted the family's return to Havana, the only thing left of the laboratory being the Brandière name in mosaic on the doorsill, dust and broken glass carpeting the once sparkling tile of the prewar lab benches. Jean took out multiple loans, got the business running again, and continued Albert's work.

Cuba now became a brothel and casino to the United States. Under the leadership of Lucky Luciano and his project manager, Meyer Lansky, Havana, a state within a state, became the playground of the Italian–American Mafia. Headquarters were at the Hotel Nacional. Over Christmas 1946, Lucky Luciano, just out of prison, organized a great gathering of the crime world there. A Bretton Woods Conference with a Mafia accent, one thousand people in attendance, including the Capone cousins Charlie, Rocco, and Joseph Fischetti, who arrived by plane with Frank Sinatra in tow. On the agenda: controlling the island's casinos, liquidating the debt-ridden Bugsy Siegel, arbitrating the struggle between Albert Anastasia and Vito Genovese — and, as a cherry on top, Lucky Luciano, *capo di tutti capi*, announced his removal to Italy, once and for all, to Naples. A prosperous and corrupt Cuba. In 1947, Fidel Castro was still a young law student, the opening gambits of the revolution were taking shape in the Dominican Republic, site of the first engagements against the dictator Trujillo. And in October 1948, Fidel married the sister of the minister of the interior, the Cuban regime's strongman, who a few years earlier had sided with the Americans against the French over control of the banana industry.

At Brandière Laboratories, the Cuban Revolution is still far in the distance. On October 27, 1949, Jenny and Françoise's trunks are loaded into a taxi bound for Orly Airport. Mother and daughter are returning to Havana.

They scan the heavens lusting for the coin
That looting the cargo bay would earn.
— Serge Gainsbourg, "Cargo Cult"

The newspaper *France-Soir* sometimes printed as many
as seven editions in a day. In the fourth edition of Friday,
October 28, 1949, Pierre Lazareff's paper publishes a special
section on the tragedy in the Azores and replays the "film
of the wait":

9:26 a.m. — *Air France announces great anxiety over the fate
of the aeroplane carrying Marcel Cerdan and thirty-six other
passengers; "Search operations were immediately undertaken by
air and sea. As of 9 a.m., nothing has been found."*

9:50 a.m. — *First detail. The Constellation transmitted its last
message at 3:55 a.m.: it was then preparing to land in the Azores.
No word has been heard since.*

10:15 a.m. — An Air France spokesman says that the loss of contact with the plane may be the result of technical difficulties: the atmospheric conditions are unfavourable to radio transmission.

10:25 a.m. — Paris is maintaining an open line with the Portuguese islands, and it can be stated with fair certainty that the plane did not land on Santa Maria.

10:50 a.m. — According to an announcement from Orly Airport, the plane went down at sea off the Azores.

11:30 a.m. — No trace of the aircraft. A slight hope survives — though the chance is slender — that the plane landed on one of the archipelago's smaller islands. It is known that at the time of its approach to the Azores airfield, the craft still had fuel for four hours of flight. Its equipment includes rubber rafts, and if it was forced down at sea the passengers and crew may yet be rescued.

12:10 p.m. — Orly announces that the plane landed seven minutes away from the Santa Maria airfield. Within minutes, Air France rebuts the statement.

1:13 p.m. — News flash: wreckage from the Paris–New York flight has been found by a search plane on the summit of Mount Algarvia, on the island of São Miguel, 75 kilometres from Santa Maria.

3 p.m. — Contradictory news: the aeroplane was observed going down in flames. But survivors have been spotted: they signalled to the pilot of the rescue plane.

+

Since first light, the aerial ballet has resumed at Orly, everyone in the crew lounge is sharing memories of the colleagues who went down in the Azores. The stewardesses talk about their friend Suzanne Roig, a great kid, tired of the business and talking about quitting it. The pilots, for their part, remember the jokes Charles Wolfer told and Raymond Redon's marriage just two weeks before to a young Algerian woman. Some still believe in a miracle, could the passengers have survived? A horde of newspapermen scavenge for the slightest quote. Henri, the barkeep at the airport, is pressed into service: "It's not possible. Just last night I brought Marcel a drink. He was in that corner of the bar, where he always sits, handing out autographs."

In the boarding area, a passenger arrives from Lydda in Palestine. His flight was held up in Rome by adverse weather, and he missed his connection to New York on the Constellation F-BAZN. He is furious, storms at the airline personnel, suddenly his anger melts away, the attendant at the boarding counter has informed him that they have no news of the Paris–New York flight of October 27.

The Air France situation room has been a hive of activity since the middle of the night. After intercepting the telegram from Portuguese aviation, the brass at the airline decide to mount their own rescue mission. The chief executive officer, Max Hymans, and the chief operating officer, Didier Daurat, choose the inspector for civil aviation,

Charles-Henri de Lévis-Mirepoix, to lead the expedition. An intimate of General de Gaulle — he was an attaché to his military cabinet in London — the duc de Lévis-Mirepoix is one of those aristocrats of the skies, a distant cousin to Captain de Boïeldieu in Renoir's *Grand Illusion*. He even has a specious resemblance to the actor Pierre Fresnay and, in the photographs that show him in uniform, wears white gloves. A few weeks earlier, he had published at Arthème Fayard a magnum opus on the history of aviation, *The Century of the Aeroplane.*

At noon, the Air France rescue mission takes off. By Lévis-Mirepoix's side are Fabre, Fournier, Marion, and Genouillac. Kept informed of developments during the flight, the French mission tries unsuccessfully to land on São Miguel Island. The airstrip is inadequate, and, at 5 p.m., the plane is forced to fall back to the airport at Santa Maria. They will have to wait a night before reaching the island where the tragedy occurred.

The first Portuguese rescuers disembark at the port of Ponta Delgada on São Miguel two hours after the announcement by the search plane. The team, reinforced by a crew of locals, proceeds to Algarvia, the village at the foot of Mount Redondo. In the early afternoon, villagers in tow, the team sets out for the crash site. The path, steep and muddy, rises some 2,600 feet before reaching the aeroplane wreck. Near the top of the peak, battered and broken, Constellation F-BAZN is still burning. The shredded sheet metal of the fuselage is strewn over the area in shapeless, calcined slabs. The Connie is nothing more than scattered metal. The fog mixes with the fire to make a single cloud, buffeted by the winds. The pulverized wings ploughed deep into the mucky soil, while the blades of the propellers, detached and lying horizontal, form the last steps to the summit. No sign of survivors anywhere in this desolate scene. The rescuers come to the bitter realization that the figures seen moving around the site earlier were looters from the village. The cargo and personal effects from the Constellation were spirited away during the morning. Last night, the peasants were roused from sleep by an explosion. Examining the sky, they saw a conflagration high on the peak. The more impetuous rushed up there in the dark.

Mount Redondo rises to an altitude of more than three thousand feet, its summit forming a kind of rounded hillock. The plane lies in the shadow of this knob. The Constellation slammed hard into the ridge top. Travelling at full speed, it burrowed in, came apart, unscrewed itself all down the slopes. Melted into the aircraft, or ejected from it, are the black and disfigured bodies. The work area is quickly cordoned off, and the Portuguese team group the passengers together on the ground. Identifying the victims proves a challenge from the start.

The sixth edition of *France-Soir* extinguishes all hope:

6:07 p.m. — Telegram from Santa Maria: "No survivors."

6:10 p.m. — According to the residents of the village of Algarvia, the aeroplane burst into flames on hitting the mountaintop.

6:13 p.m. — It is now certain that a major disaster has occurred. Air France has just announced, "The rescue teams have reached the wreck; there are no survivors."

That night, Prince Aly Khan of Pakistan, the husband of Rita Hayworth, narrowly escapes an aeroplane accident. The plane makes an emergency landing on the Croydon airfield, in the suburbs of London, shortly after taking off from there. It lands without mishap using a single engine. Aly Khan immediately boards another plane.

12 The Five-Millionth Mickey Mouse Watch

When trains derail, what upsets me are the dead in first class.
— Salvador Dalí

In a letter to the vice president of his company mailed on Wednesday, October 26, 1949, the day before his trip, Kay Kamen joked with his close colleague about his aeroplane phobia. It was a long-standing source of amusement to them, given how seriously the businessman suffered from aviophobia, or acrophobia, as the doctors variously called it. The Superga tragedy on May 4, 1949, had done nothing to reassure him. The aircraft, a Fiat G.212, crashed into the Basilica of Superga on a ridge above the Po River Valley, and the entire Torino football team had been killed. Some of the most famous players of the postwar years, just after winning their fifth *scudetto*. A tragedy for the *tifosi* of Turin and for Italy as a whole.

But for Kamen it was more a topic for jokes than a real handicap in his work. His business came first, and any fears came afterwards. Had he not bet his career on a poker hand one morning in July 1932, laying fifty thousand dollars on the desk of a certain Walt Disney as though on the green baize of a casino table? He was a man of shadow, but what a shadow, the king of merchandising, the inventor of one of the most profitable economic models of the twentieth century: the marketing of products derived from cartoon characters. A small gruff man, hiding his game behind heavy-framed round glasses, giving himself an air of seriousness and, paradoxically, of whimsicality by parting his hair impeccably down the middle. Thanks to his business sense, he had been the lucky charm, the saviour, of the Disney brothers, their Jiminy Cricket.

Kamen gained his business sense through experience. His first big commercial deal had been merchandising products derived from a successful series of short films from the 1920s, Hal Roach's *Our Gang*, or *The Little Rascals*. The story revolved around a gang of poor children, with Spanky, the fat kid, as their leader. His followers included the wire-thin Alfalfa; pretty Darla; Porky, the youngest; his sidekick, Buckwheat; and their pit bull terrier, Pete. The series had the great virtue of showing children in their natural state and avoiding the stereotypes of the time. Kay Kamen used *Our Gang* to develop the basic strategy that would reach its zenith a few years later with the merchandizing of Disney characters and was able to turn the success of these short films into profit. The many derivative products included figurines of the characters, lunch boxes, pencil cases, school bags, comic strips, magazines, even candies—there was a Spanky candy bar and Little Rascals chewing gum. The fact that so many children in America identified with Roach's scoundrelly kids made them a great moneymaker.

+

Like many Americans, Kay lost just about everything during the Wall Street crash of 1929. A salesman in New York once more, he became interested in the early work of the Disney studios. Walt Disney had been on a train between New York and Los Angeles a year earlier when he had imagined a mouse with big ears, first known as "Mortimer Mouse", later to become "Mickey Mouse". The studio's iconic character would make his first public appearance, together with Minnie Mouse and Black Pete, at the Colony Theatre on Broadway on November 18, 1928, at the premiere of *Steamboat Willie*, the first animated film with synchronized sound. Seven minutes, during which the rodent lifts Minnie on board by the seat of her trousers using a crane, swings a cat by the tail, strangles a goose, and transforms three little piglets attached to their mother's teats into an ingenious piano. New characters would follow, first Pluto the Pup, then Donald Duck. Mickey Mouse was exported, becoming Topolino in Italy and Miki Kuchi in Japan. Technicolor would revolutionize the world of animation, and Walt secured exclusive rights to the process for two years. In 1932, his Silly Symphonies short *Flowers and Trees* won the Oscar for Best Animated Short, and Walt won an honorary Oscar for creating Mickey Mouse. From then on, although it continued to operate in the red, the studio towered as the symbol of the burgeoning entertainment industry. The sale of products derived from the company was still in its infancy. Kay Kamen's arrival would lead to the explosive growth of merchandizing and transform the studio into an empire.

In July 1932, when Kamen forced his way past the Disney brothers' door, he played his last card. A hand of double or nothing. The biggest bluff of his career, an insane contract: the studio would receive a guaranteed income of fifty thousand dollars a year that would cost Disney not a cent, in return for which Kamen would get half of any hypothetical future profits from merchandizing. An offer they couldn't refuse. To pull it off, Kamen had cashed in his life insurance and mortgaged his house. Once he had his ante, he hopped on the first train to Hollywood without buying a ticket. For four days he sat on the train and rehearsed his argument, with ample time to imagine his listeners' reactions, shore up his position, and invent a confidence for himself that would convince the brothers to sign on. That it was sure to be financially successful in no way changed the fact that the whole business was based on chance. He knew it. And made every effort to hide the anxiety that flooded him. The contracts had been solidly prepared beforehand, with the studio insured against any and all risk, in return for exclusive rights to license Disney-derived products. Without an appointment, he cooled his heels for several days in the reception area before the doors magically opened. Kay entered the Disney brothers' office on July 1, his future in his attaché case, all staked on a pair of signatures. After the usual formalities, he traded on surprise and, while describing his project, produced the contract and the fifty thousand dollars in cash. A few minutes later, the three men signed and drank a toast to their partnership.

Having obtained exclusive rights, the Kay Kamen Company sorted through the existing licensing agreements and started in earnest to market products relating to the studio. The gamble was a good one, since, as of Christmas 1932, Kay Kamen was able to pay his astonished partners $2.5 million in licensing royalties and, by the terms of the contract, pocket the same sum himself. A brilliant success, owed to the launch that August of Mickey Mouse ice-cream cones. By the end of the summer, ten million cones had been sold. The brazen bluff proved a gold-plated masterstroke, and *Citizen Kay* was off and running. That same summer, while gawkers licked their ice creams, a great fire at the corner of Boardwalk and Surf Avenues devastated Coney Island. Clustered on the beach, thousands of holidaymakers silently watched the blaze that kids scratching matches had set off.

The man Walt Disney was starting to call "MicKay Kamen" was not about to stop in mid-stride. In 1933, at his urging, *Mickey Mouse Magazine* began publication. The monthly, supported by dairy producers, was distributed in movie theatres and department stores, generating an unexpected windfall of publicity. Kamen made use of every opportunity, and although the Great Depression made millions of Americans homeless, he dreamed up the most profitable commercial project in the studio's history: the Mickey Mouse watch. The businessman drew the initial sketch for the prototype himself. The mouse painted at the centre of the dial would tell the time with his big, gloved hands, the minutes and seconds intersecting, in effect animating the character. Three small mice at Mickey's feet would serve as a stopwatch. The idea was sold to the Ingersoll–Waterbury Clock Company, an organization that had been hit hard by the financial crisis and was, in 1933, on the brink of bankruptcy. The Mickey Mouse watch saved the company. Its success was unprecedented. In its first year of production, eleven thousand watches were sold at Macy's department store in New York City. By 1935, 2.5 million Mickey Mouse watches had been manufactured, and Ingersoll paid Disney nearly $250,000 in royalties. Kamen, strapping a watch to the wrist of millions of American children, was responding in his own way to Herbert Hoover's promise to put a chicken in every pot. And with his licensing system, he specialized in saving companies from bankruptcy. A windup Disney train toy, offered for a dollar from railroad maintenance cars, helped set the Lionel Corporation back on its feet. Catalogs issued by the businessman during the holiday season also contributed to the exponential growth of Disney products. The merchandizing campaigns Kamen

dreamed up got results, even promoting the studio's cartoon characters. His Three Little Pigs and Big Bad Wolf
puppets, for instance, were the best-selling toys of 1934.
The Kay Kamen Company was growing, and Kamen was
extending his reach. Seizing on the worldwide success of
Snow White, he had his catalogue translated into nineteen
languages. A modest investment, considering the profits
generated a few months later by the sale of licensing agreements abroad. At the release of each new feature, the same
commercial strategy was deployed: sweets, dolls, clothing,
and toys based on the characters filled the pages of the
sales catalog. In 1938, royalties for the dwarf Dopey alone
generated hundreds of thousands of dollars.

Only World War II slowed Disney's rising power. The
company built on its popularity by taking part in the war
effort. On July 14, 1942, the studios — in collaboration with
Lockheed Aircraft (the company that would build the Constellation) — released a cartoon on techniques for riveting
aeroplanes, an instruction manual in the form of a short
animated film, *Four Methods of Flush Riveting*, aimed at the
government's civilian contractors. Animators who had been
drafted into the armed services made cartoons for military use throughout the war — on subjects from small-arms
handling to military strategy — as well as propaganda films,
with titles like *Der Fuehrer's Face* and *Victory Through Air
Power*. Disney's enlistment in the war effort came about by

chance, an odd fate for a studio whose releases were highly prized by the Axis dictators: Didn't Hitler consider *Snow White* a masterpiece? Had he not drawn admiring copies of the seven dwarves and Pinocchio? And didn't Mussolini invite Walt Disney to the Villa Torlonia in 1935 to discuss *The Three Little Pigs* and Mickey Mouse?

The postwar world saw the unstoppable rise of the Disney studios and, with them, of Kay Kamen's business. In 1947, the Walt Disney Company recorded revenues of $1,048,522 just from merchandizing. Walt never missed an opportunity to congratulate himself on his partnership with Kay Kamen and praise the former salesman's loyalty and genius. In 1949, Disney organized a grand occasion to mark the five-millionth Mickey Mouse watch, but all the hoopla hid the Disney brothers' intention to gradually sever their ties with the Kay Kamen Company. A few weeks before the October 27 flight, Disney balked at renewing a contract that Kamen considered a lock because of the revenues it generated. Heated negotiations followed, aimed at restricting Kamen's field of action to the domestic U.S. market. During the long hours of bargaining, Kamen had the bitter sense of being betrayed by the very people he had so often saved from bankruptcy. Others had laid the groundwork, and now Disney was looking to maximize its revenues. Kamen was the one caught in the wringer.

When he travels to Paris with his wife, Ketty, in October 1949 to promote merchandise for the animated feature

Cinderella, the new conditions of his partnership have not yet been agreed on. Negotiations will resume on his return and must at all costs be concluded before the start of 1950. Fate would have it otherwise. A few weeks later, the studio decides to create a new division, Disney Consumer Products, which will handle merchandizing internally.

At a dinner at Warner Bros. in 1945, Walt Disney invites Salvador Dalí to make a short animated film along the lines of *Fantasia* to be called *Destino* (Fate). The story of the love of Chronos, the god of time, for a mortal woman, summed up by Walt in one sentence: "A simple story about a young girl in search of true love." Intrigued by the idea, Dalí sees it as a way to animate the world of his paintings, to set in motion the labyrinth of time, as he would write. For nearly eight months, the painter goes regularly to the Disney studios, where he works with the art director John Hench on developing the short film. The project was eventually dropped, proving too costly and esoteric. What remains of it are a few sketches, a storyboard in which a woman wafts, to an Andalusian score, through the paintings of Dalí, endless deserts populated by surrealist gods and strewn with soft clocks. Can we see among them one of the five million Mickey Mouse watches, broken and dripping on the carcass of a Constellation, like *The Persistence of Memory* draped over *Destino*?

13   On the Slopes of Redondo

A pile of rubble randomly heaped:
the most beautiful order in the world.
—Heraclitus, *Fragments*

At first light, the French mission, led by the inspector of
civil aviation, Lévis-Mirepoix, boards an island hopper at
the Santa Maria airfield for the flight to Ponta Delgada.
The Portuguese authorities have given orders to leave the
wreckage of the Constellation undisturbed at the crash
site until the designated commission arrives. Three hours
later, joined by the British and American consuls, the
team starts up from the foot of Mount Redondo. Under
a steady rain, along slippery paths coated in sticky and
unstable mud, the investigators begin the long climb
towards the crash. After several hours of walking, they
reach the aircraft and meet with the team of local rescuers sent the day before. The disaster area, covering sixty
acres, is cloaked in a mantle of thick fog, lapped with

damp, milky folds. Flames have consumed the debris and scattered it to the four winds, and aside from five more or less recognizable corpses it seems impossible at first sight to identify the Constellation's victims from the various limbs distributed among the rocks. The aeroplane lies broken, its aluminium carapace — twisted, dismembered, and grimy from the flames — has lost its bright metal reflection. Part of the fuselage, open at the roof and sunk into the ground, seems almost intact, a sectional plan of F-BAZN, in which, strapped to their seats, a dozen passengers remain. The conic tail section, planted vertically, looms over the archipelago like the *Winged Victory of Samothrace*. Farther along, the overturned cockpit, which rolled until it wedged itself against the rock, seems to maintain itself by levitation. The flight crew is recognizable inside from the fragments of their uniforms. Only the face of the third pilot, Camille Fidency, is intact. Like a cast from Pompeii, the young man shields his eyes from the imminent disaster with a raised forearm.

After a methodical and exhausting search, the mission discovers something a few dozen yards away. Near the corpse of a young woman, her crimson dress burned at the armholes, lies an open violin case containing a broken bow. They immediately connect it with the body of the violinist Ginette Neveu, but the inference is based only on proximity. Farther on, a cellophane envelope protects the identity card of Jo Longman, Marcel Cerdan's manager, but no nearby corpse can be attached to it. Bending to their task, the French photographers snap their Rolleiflexes at the wreckage, while in the camera chamber, mediated by the lens, disparate pieces of the Constellation emerge. The wrinkled sheet metal underfoot in checkerboard-sized pieces looks, from a slight distance, like a collapsed house of cards. The slopes of Redondo are strewn with jewels, banknotes, gutted trunks vomiting their contents, and stray objects of value, separated from their owners and overlooked by the looters. Between two shrubs, a brown leather billfold, the property of an American citizen, John Abbott. Here, a swatch of green cloth, and there, not far away, the dress it came from, draping the wounded legs of yet another corpse. Over there, a bullfinch pecks at a fern's sporangium, and on the mountainside, nestled on the sea-green moss, an arm.

From disorder can emerge a troubling beauty. A bee swarm, the monads spreading through the air compose, recompose, and decompose, in pointillist style, an apparently chaotic painting. Leibniz, defending the harmony of God's plan, resorted to a painterly metaphor. Suppose, said the philosopher, that you are standing in front of a magnificent painting covered by an opaque veil in such a way that you see only a tiny portion of it; this portion will no doubt seem a blotch of shapeless colour, an absurd smear randomly applied to the canvas; but remove the veil and what has seemed inchoate will suddenly make sense and reveal the maker's artistry. The blotch is ugly only when perceived in isolation and separated from all of which it forms a part. Its ugliness is not objective, but the effect of a blinkered view, and it disappears as soon as the part is brought into relation with the whole. Chaos is a matter of scale, and, from a man's height, the smouldering peak—like the opaque veil in Leibniz's *Theodicy*—hides the perspective of a planned order.

+

The rescue team continues reconstructing the puzzle of Constellation F-BAZN. From a solid, gleaming, and aero-dynamic body, the plane has been dispersed into a heap of sheet metal plates. The cloying smell of burnt rubber swirls and mixes in the fine mist, the charred residue floats to form a thin, blackish layer on the rescuers' clothing. Small objects, initially overlooked, now make it possible to put names to disjointed corpses. By nightfall, forty victims have been identified. Among the puzzle pieces randomly spilled out, a watch strapped to a corpse's wrist establishes the owner's identity. An "M" and a "C" engraved on the back fairly shout Marcel Cerdan's name. The stopped hands indicate ten minutes to nine, as though they had continued turning for six hours, despite the brutal impact. But the explanation is completely different, the hands show when the crash occurred in U.S. time. Day for night. The watch had progressed beyond its own fate. The boxer wore not one but two watches, one set to Paris time, the other, a Reflet by Boucheron, set to New York time. It was a present from Édith Piaf, a good-luck charm.

+

The victims' remains are covered in tent canvas, and the lit-
ters are carried down the mountain in procession. The rescuers stumble, slide on the viscous ground, the repatriation
turns into a prolonged stations of the cross. The hurricane
lanterns cast their smoky yellow light on the night watch.
After a long section through a dense forest of cypresses, the
valley opens out, the village of Algarvia is at the bottom.
The bodies are laid one after another on the flagstones of
the little church in the village centre. As they are identified, they are placed in lead-lined whitewood coffins. In the
spring, the church's baroque façade is repainted in bright
colours. On this All Hallows' Eve, the headlights sweep
across the building to reveal the weathered paint from last
Pentecost. A first funeral vigil is organized. In the nave, by
the light of candles and storm lanterns, the inhabitants of
the village file past the victims to the continuous murmur
of the Paternoster. The Portuguese prayers of the shepherds and their wives weave a long lament, *"Dai-lhes Senhor
o eterno descanso"* (Give them, O Lord, eternal rest).

14 *Arista's Prophecy*

I know that people die
By chance
Just lengthening their stride.

—Jacques Brel, *"La ville s'endormait"* ("The Town Fell Asleep")

She had called, the Little Sparrow. In New York, with Marcel far away, she was dying of boredom and grief. She begged him over the phone to move up his date of departure, she couldn't take it, she told him over and over. And why oblige her to suffer when nothing could be easier than to squeeze a few extra days out of the schedule by exchanging the slow boat for an express trip on the Constellation? Jo Longman, his manager, had groused like hell, but here they are driving the blue Pontiac to the airport. It will be up to Jo to wangle three last-minute seats on Air France's F-BAZN. Despite the hurried departure, Marcel insists that they stop the car at L'Ambassade des Opéras on the rue Saint-Anne, the bar that serves as the gang's headquarters, to say good-bye to the girls, Mado and Irène, and Jacquot the barman, and Néné. The day before, they'd been in Troyes for an exhibition match at the municipal amphitheatre. Cerdan had promised to go three rounds with the golden boy of French boxing, Valère Benedetto, from Aix. He'd kept his word, and the cream of the Paris sporting world had travelled to the provincial city to see Cerdan climb into the ring one last time before his big fight with Jake LaMotta. Afterwards, at the restaurant Aux Vins de Bourgogne, he said in his reedy voice: "I want to fight him and reclaim my title, and I'll beat him." A child's voice, high-pitched and awkward, that jarred with his boxy frame and champion's record. Comparable in strangeness to the brawling Blaise Cendrars's fluty countertenor.

After his victory, Jake LaMotta had played hard-to-get. The Mafia's protégé first cancelled the return match, set for September 28, claiming an injury to his right shoulder. It took Jo Longman endless negotiations to get a new date from his impresarios, December 2, 1949, at Madison Square Garden. Marcel had his revenge within reach of his fists. He imagined himself battering his opponent with blows, trapping him against the ropes, making him pay for his disrespect with devastating combinations to his kidneys and chin. At the sound of the bell, he would erupt from his corner, throw himself on LaMotta, and knock him to the canvas. Not the shadow of a doubt. The great matadors are haunted by bulls they have faced. Toreros gone mad, they wake in the middle of the night, visited (or so they say) by a white bull. Some, according to legend, are discovered half-asleep, sword drawn, citing the bull that watches them from the corner of the room. Night terror, fatal omen. Marcel dreamed several times of the rematch. The ring is in the middle of an ancient arena. LaMotta watches him, takes his measure, dances, taunts him. The rounds go by, and Marcel can't find the opening he needs, the deft feints of the Raging Bull confuse, exhaust him. Then, in the fifth round, always the fifth, he contains the white bull's charge, upsets his timing, cuts his legs from under him, locks him between his two fists. An ideally placed right hook disorients his opponent, then two more shatter his wavering guard, two steps to the side and a swift uppercut, the death blow. Knocked to the canvas, LaMotta does not get up. To his daily training, Marcel adds the mental performance of this cathartic shadowboxing.

+

If only it were just LaMotta. If only Édith would show some patience. Boxing has its rules, and sometimes they are biased, but when you have a knockout, the hands go up, there's no contesting it. Since he met Piaf, he has had to lie, make promises and retractions, advance and retreat, manage one woman, calm the other, the game is beyond him. In July, while he was at the Loch Sheldrake training camp near New York, training for the September match, Édith on a tour of North Africa spent three days in Casablanca. On his side of the Atlantic, three days of anxiety that she was going to have an apoplectic fit. His brother, Armand, was standing in for him, but he couldn't protect Marcel from a scandal. A July 23 letter from Édith only partially reassured him. She was insisting that he make a choice:

> *My love,*
>
> *There, I've opened in Casablanca. The newspaper coverage really hurt me. First, we had to turn people away, and then I sang only fourteen songs. People thought it wasn't very many, and I was genuinely afraid the Miami would collapse from all the foot stamping. Your brother Armand was there and his wife. I should warn you, his wife said to me, "I like you a lot, and I didn't expect you to be pretty." So, if she runs into your wife, that should make her happy. Anyway, the newspapers also wrote that I was pretty, tough luck for you. I'm proud for your sake, my love, I'd like to be the prettiest of them all, the most perfect, so that the day will never come when you stop loving me. That's why I am making myself more beautiful and improving my mind. You're so perfect and I want so much to be like you.*
>
> *I heard that you're going to build a villa in Casablanca for 10 million and that every time you come back here you settle in a little more. Sweetheart, that's what kills me and makes me feel I don't understand anything. Listen, I'm going to tell you something that may open your eyes. You know I've never gotten involved in any of this, but now I've got*

to speak out, because everyone comes to me saying that if I love you, I should open your eyes and put you on your guard. Darling, you need to make a decision, first for the children's sake, and then for your own. You're their father, and you also have to defend them. After your fight in September, you owe it to yourself to take stern measures on behalf of your kids. For my part, I'm going to suggest something that is perfectly feasible, something that will make both your kids and you happy. I'm going to nag you until you do something about it. You're going to be astonished by all that I'm going to teach you. But now I know why God set me on your path, He would never have allowed me to do anything bad, and that's why all the coincidences that surround us, which we find so astonishing, are not coincidences but signs from heaven that I should never leave you. And I'm sure that LaMotta is a call from God telling me to always be near you. Every time we are apart, you get a hard knock. Look at Delannoit and LaMotta. Then look at Zale, Turpin, Roach, you knocked all those guys out the same way. I am sure now that God wants me to be near you, as sure as I live. And I'll tell you about other things that are so amazing it sometimes sends chills down my spine! I love you and my love is so strong that it protects you!

. . . I'm so happy to love you the way I do. Only twelve days and I'll be able to touch you and kiss you as I want.

Your own tiny tiny

+

In August on the Côte d'Azur, and then on the ocean liner *Île de France*, he had sworn that he would make a decision after his victory. He would stop his career, have the time to think. Step back before taking a leap. Then the news came, the match was delayed.

Marcel Cerdan, ensconced with his family near Casablanca, was killing time, hanging on LaMotta's decision. Marinette was there, his three children, his brother Armand, and his nephew René, who had become his sparring partner. He bounced between the farm at Sidi Maârouf, the villa under construction at Ansa, and the ASPTT boxing gym, where he practised his scales. Batting rhythmically at the leather hide of the speedball. Bif, baf, bif. Harder, left, right, left, punish that punching bag, whumpf, whumpf, whumpf. The jump rope snicks against the wooden floor, whack, whack, whack.

Marcel had trouble accepting the fact that he'd been taken by an outsider who came out of nowhere, out of the pocket of some Cosa Nostra godfather. A bitter-tasting defeat to the world's tenth-ranked middleweight, a confluence of events that were suspect, to say the least, and had erased any possibility of victory. At Briggs Stadium in Detroit, on June 16, 1949, the bout had been moved forward half an hour. Marcel was unable to complete his ritual warm-up before entering the ring. Cold, he slipped in the first round, dislocating his right shoulder, and was forced to absorb the epileptic flurries of the Bronx Bull. It hadn't been a washout. LaMotta had battered his tender shoulder until the pain was unbearable. In the eleventh round, pressured by his cornermen, the Frenchman conceded.

He knew that at full capacity he was unbeatable. And the Cerdan flying toward the United States in October 1949 was at the top of his form. "Today, defeat is unthinkable. I have to beat LaMotta, I'm going to beat him. I'll be perfect on December 2. Believe me, I'll return to France with the world middleweight crown firmly on my head," he told a journalist from *France-Soir*.

In the departure hall at Orly, Marcel is wearing his lucky blue suit. Over it, further bulking up his giant frame, is a heavy grey tweed coat. The boxer is superstitious and has his habits, never departing from them in the ring or out. In fact, he blames his defeat in Detroit a few months earlier on the disruption to his ritual. If the conditions for his ritual preparation had been respected, if he had been able to warm up as he'd planned, his shoulder would have been fine, and they wouldn't be facing a return match today. Instead he'd be defending an inviolate title. Athletes give inordinate importance to these details, which allow them to contain the unpredictable within a series of well-determined causes. If fate can't be absolutely mastered, then at least let's ensure the lead-up, encase the details of preparation inside a subjective magic, a prematch paganism. Crazy tics, raised to the level of ceremonial rites, some might say. But adhering rigidly to details is not more odd than using a thousand-year-old liturgy that has hardened into dogma. Ordained a champion, you must never fail in observing the religion you have settled on yourself. Since his first professional fights in Levallois, Marcel has worn the blue trunks with the white stripe that his mother made for him, sewing a medal of the baby Jesus between two tucks. And only by winding the ACE bandages just so can you conjure victory.

Despite his superstition, Marcel Cerdan paid no attention to Arista's prophecy. The famous fortune-teller met the boxer at Paul Genser's apartment on the rue d'Orsel in early October. Tickled, Marcel took part in the game. Laying his two big hands on the table, upturned, he exposed the deep creases across his palms. Cartography of a life, traced by furrows in the skin, where the crisscrossing lines of heart, head, fate, and luck reveal, by their branching and interconnection, the ineluctable workings of providence. Pausing at the mound of Saturn below the index finger, symbol of good or bad luck, Arista delivered a lapidary prophecy that echoed like a warning: "You travel too often by aeroplane, be careful." Jo Longman, sitting at the back of the room, dispelled the ominous forecast with his laughter and, imitating the fortune-teller's voice, predicted that Cerdan would soon meet a man-bull, a kind of Minotaur, whom he would knock to the ground, and he added that, Theseus-like, he would emerge from the labyrinth of New York with an Ariadne called Édith on his arm and that the prophecy would come true on his return, when, like Icarus, he would perish from his flight. The augury was buried under general hilarity. The next day, Arista, troubled by his prophecy, asked for and insisted on getting the boxer's birth record, so as to draw up an accurate horoscope. A week later, Marcel received a letter with a second warning: "Avoid air travel, especially on Fridays."

The lesson of Cassandra is that the more specifically an oracle speaks, the less she is listened to. And if a prophecy is heard and heeded, every action taken to ward it off helps bring it about. To struggle, to reverse course, is all part of the game, that's the lesson of the oracle at Delphi. In short, no one escapes his fate.

"Take the plane, the boat is too slow!" Édith pleaded over the telephone the day before. The Constellation crossed the Atlantic on Thursday night and arrived in New York the next morning. He could come and wake her up, they would spend the day together, and that night he would hear her sing at the Versailles. The prophecy is forgotten. Marinette calls a few minutes before the flight to tell him she has a bad feeling, is anxious. He has never known her to have such fears. He reassures her. Meanwhile, Jo Longman wrests three seats from the Air France receptionists, even though the flight is full. The world champion deserves to take precedence all the same, which he does at the expense of Mme Erdmann, director of a perfume company, and a young American couple who have been honeymooning in Paris. At the airport bar, his sidekicks to the right and left of him, Marcel drinks to his comeback.

"LaMotta has got it coming to him for stealing my title!"

15 *Ponta Delgada*

Below the kirk, below the hill,
Below the lighthouse top.
— Samuel Taylor Coleridge, "The Rime of the Ancient Mariner"

During the night of Sunday to Monday, a final expedition ascends Mount Redondo in search of the last victims of the Constellation, over which three infantrymen from the local barracks stand guard. At midnight, the rescuers bring the remains back to the village. The hamlet is under siege, the traffic of military vehicles blocks the only street and carves deep ruts in the ground. Housed in the presbytery adjoining the church, the members of the Air France commission gather their notes and draft their first reports. Hundreds of details, which they match with the typed passenger list. Their first priority is to attach a name to each corpse before it is transferred to Ponta Delgada. The technical report on the accident's causes can wait. What do they feel, these men at the forefront of the disaster? Discouragement at the sheer size of the job? Weariness from a day at the centre of the volcano, grubbing through and analysing the smouldering entrails of the Constellation? Anger that the site was looted?

Lévis-Mirepoix wants to start tracking down the looters immediately. At dawn, the commissioners inspect the houses in Algarvia, questioning the inhabitants. A pearl necklace and wedding rings turn up here, a wad of dollar bills there. And what to make of the woman they stop in the street wrapped in a fur coat? At some distance from the village, along a path, the sounds of a violin rise from a shack. They knock on the door, the noise stops, an old man opens, holding his instrument and a bow trimmed with tortoise shell and gold.

— Is this yours?

— No, I found it, the man answers.

The bow, a "Fleur-de-Lys" model, bears the mark of W. E. Hill & Sons, the famous London violin makers. The commissioners immediately confiscate the bow, the violin—an old one—stays with the countryman.

At noon, the army organizes the removal of the coffins to the base at Ponta Delgada. Four trucks serve as hearses, trundling along the hairpin road that separates Algarvia from the Santana airfield. Two hours later, the coffins sit on benches in the dining hall of the whitewashed barracks. It is Monday, October 31, the row of unlabelled coffins, decorated with wreaths and garlands, and the improvised altar give the infantry canteen the aspect of a morgue. Ponta Delgada is the capital of São Miguel. Known as "Ilha Verde", the island at one time was a reprovisioning point for caravels between Europe and the New World, a bustling hub. The Praça Gonçalo Velho Cabral, ringed on four sides by arcades, marks the last terrestrial gate to the sea with three proud arches. The walls of the Forte de São Bras beetle over the citadel. On the fifth Sunday after Easter, the residents strew the flagstones of the city with island flowers. They celebrate the Holy Ghost, and a procession forms behind an enormous Christ made of painted ebony, splashed with gold and diamonds. In the parish church, the gathered crowd consecrates a child as emperor, on his head the magnificent crown, in his hand the hundred-year-old sceptre. The baby-king files out and opens the festivities.

What wood are the coffins in the barracks made of, wood from the vast forests in the vale at the centre of the island? That afternoon, the absolution of the dead is performed by the priest of Ponta Delgada. Present are the civil governor, the chief local authorities, the members of the Air France mission. The coffins are grouped by nationality, some draped in the Union Jack, some in the Stars and Stripes. The French will have to await the arrival of Consul Morin, presently in Lisbon. After the Catholic service, a Protestant American chaplain in an air-force uniform reads out verses from the Old Testament. Outside, the flags on the base are flying at half-mast, Portuguese soldiers march at attention in front of a double row of schoolchildren, dressed all in white.

Lévis-Mirepoix speaks that night with Didier Merlin of *Le Figaro* and reports on the early stages of the investigation: "It's still too early to draw conclusions from the elements we've gathered. Every member of the commission, coordinating, of course, with the others, has conducted his own inquiry, in the area assigned to him by his specialty. We have been accompanied by representatives of the flight personnel: a pilot, a radio operator, a navigator, and a mechanic, charged with gathering information relative to their roles when flying. We have not yet been able to examine the information we have gathered. Each of us holds a piece of the puzzle that makes up the disaster, but will it not always be a riddle, even when all the pieces have been assembled? The aircraft, as you know, crashed into the mountain on the side of Mount Redondo, between Redondo and Algarvia Peak, the highest on the island of São Miguel, thirty miles from wider, flatter ground that might be considered a small pass."

I remember that Ginette Neveu died
in the same aeroplane as Marcel Cerdan.
— Georges Perec, *I Remember*

Encircling the advertising columns along Paris's boulevards, posters for the Salle Pleyel theatre announce in capital letters and in Indian file:

PRIOR TO HER DEPARTURE

GINETTE NEVEU

WILL PERFORM A FAREWELL CONCERT

THURSDAY OCTOBER 20

AT THE SALLE PLEYEL

On the programme for this last turn at the violin before the Americas, Handel's Sonata in D Major, Bach's Chaconne in D Minor for solo violin, Szymanowski's *Nocturne and Tarantella*, and Ravel's *Pièce en forme de Habanera* and *Tzigane*.

Her long pink gown framing her gladiator's shoulders, Ginette Neveu, accompanied on the piano by her brother, Jean, bows her instrument for an hour without letup, her impeccable interpretation of the repertoire both nimble and passionate. The public has come to hear this prodigy, this Mozart in a dress, whose praises the whole world is singing. Especially to hear her *Tzigane*, encored after each movement as usual, an eight snaking around a caduceus. In Paris, between two concerts, Ginette remains closeted in the family apartment on the square Henri-Delormel. Endless hours spent rehearsing the programme, bringing the slightest detail to perfection, digging to the edge of madness for the right interpretation. Then, in the early light, walking the broad avenues, strolling in the hour between dog and wolf among the invisible fraternity of lone early birds. At the age of ten, she wrote in a composition: "Even better are the Champs-Elysées when the cool morning air and glorious light make for an indefinable grandeur, one that you don't experience during the day. The few out walking aren't speaking, they are contemplating... But in two hours, the pedants will have retaken possession of the avenues, the enchantment will be gone."

That morning, she sees the great posters to her glory. In one stroke of the paperhanger's brush, a SOLD OUT strip extends across each ad. Ginette chose her fate. It is easy to attach the label "prodigy" to her precocious career and miss, through facile stereotyping, the child's implacable will, hard work, and discipline, the mailed fist of her genius.

A staccato like no other, fruit of the obstinacy of a serious child. We like fairy tales, Newton's apple, eureka moments, grace conceived as a punctual, innate, and ineluctable event, and we erase, because of our penchant for the marvellous, the prior groundwork, the tedious chores, the doubts. At seven, after a first concert at the Salle Gaveau, Ginette trains hard to overcome her anxiety, stop the trembling in her knees, conquer the sweat on her forehead and palms. In the evening, standing on the kitchen table practising, she tells her astonished mother: "It's to get used to performing onstage. The other day, I had stage fright, it was probably vertigo."

An Armistice baby, Ginette Neveu is born in 1919 in Paris. Her mother, a piano teacher, introduces her to music early. Ginette watches the students come and go from a corner of the living room and, at eleven months, hums the melodies she has heard. Passersby stare at this baby carriage rocked by its own lullabies. At two, she attends a concert in tribute to Frédéric Chopin, on the way home, in tears, she is heard to say, "How much feeling he shows! Oh, how unhappy that man must have been!" Her first violin, quarter-sized, is presented to her when she turns five, and her parents enrol her, on the advice of Professeur Nadaud of the Paris Conservatory, to take courses with Mme Talluel. In no time at all, staccato, spiccato, jeté bowing, sautillé hold no secrets for her. On the evidence of her unusual maturity, six months after starting to study violin, Ginette gives her first public recital, performing a Schumann fugue. She receives her first applause, which she doesn't understand, and, after a curtsy, she imitates the audience's clapping. Two years later, Ginette shines at the Salle Gaveau, she gives a brilliant performance of Max Bruch's Concerto no. 1 in G Minor. Outside, a violent storm crashes down, she doesn't hear the noise. To her mother, surprised at her unflappable aplomb, she answers: "Thunder? There was a storm?"

Ginette Neveu's voice, like Marcel Cerdan's, is a paradox. Marcel, wrapped in a giant's body, talks like a shy boy, stuttering, stumbling over his words, having to force the thin stream of his voice higher to be heard, he is a soprano. Ginette, a child-adult, projects her confidence, her certainty at having been chosen, in a deep voice, fixing you with her bottomless eyes, imposing rather than proposing, she is a contralto. Interrupted in the middle of the Bach Chaconne by the maestro George Enescu, who suggests that she replay a passage, she answers, "I do what I understand, not what escapes me." In November 1930, at eleven, she is admitted to the National Conservatory of Music. She follows Jules Boucherit's class for just eight months before receiving the first prize for violin, matching the feat achieved by Wieniawski. A year later, she enters her first international contest in Vienna against 250 violinists twice her age and reaches the finals. On the jury is Carl Flesch, who is so impressed by the child's technique and inspiration that he leaves a message at the hotel for her mother:

"If you can arrange to come to Berlin, I will undertake to look after the young violinist entirely pro bono." It would take the family two years to find the money for the trip. In the meantime, Ginette meets Nadia Boulanger and, for her own amusement, composes three sonatas for solo violin, a capriccio, and the beginnings of a concerto for violin and orchestra. In March 1935, at sixteen, she comes to international attention by winning first prize in the Wieniawski Violin Competition, judged by David Oistrakh. After the award ceremony, she writes a letter to Mme Talluel:

> *My Dear Professor,*
>
> *I am rushing to announce to you the happy news: after taking first place in the first examination, I have just won first prize in the second round. I don't need to tell you how happy this has made my mother and me too. Unfortunately, the rules oblige me to stay another month in Poland to give concerts. The session ended last night at 2 a.m., I played my concerto very well...*
>
> *I have therefore received... wait for it... a diploma, a check, a silver cup that belonged to Wieniawski, and a strange violin that looks like a mandolin!!*

Ginette Neveu is discovering the world. Between 1935 and 1939, she tours in Poland, the United Kingdom, throughout the USSR, and in Canada and the United States, everywhere drawing the same acclaim. She reportedly says: "Now I'm really going to have to work!"

Then comes the Phoney War, the French surrender, the cutting off of the occupied countries. Ginette goes into internal exile. She plays only the small concert halls in France's southern Free Zone, and, despite lucrative offers from the Nazi government in Germany, she declines to play in Berlin and Stuttgart. During her impromptu tours through the French countryside, overnighting in train station hotels and sleeping berths, she is joined by her brother, Jean Neveu. As the one exception to her musical resistance movement, she accepts a concert at the Salle Gaveau on January 19, 1943, performing concertos by Bach, Beethoven, and Brahms. Her friendship with the composer Francis Poulenc dates from this concert, and he would later dedicate a sonata to her.

June 1944, the Allied landing. As the troops advance, Ginette performs more widely. Belgium is liberated, she goes to Brussels and gives a fiery concert. She then takes the first train to Switzerland; stopped at the border, she nonetheless slips in. A journalist for *La Feuille d'avis de Lausanne* accompanies her and tells the story:

> At the border, a resourceful stationmaster couples a special car to the back of a freight train to allow these unexpected travellers to pass. The engineer, who can't shake his surprise, gets out at every stop to make sure that his travellers are happy, entertains them with conversation, brings them newspapers. In this way, Ginette Neveu abruptly learns from a press report that a replacement has been found for her and that she won't be

playing at the Geneva Symphony Orchestra concert: they believe it will be impossible for her to get through. Revealing her identity, she leaps to the telephone at the next station, sets the record straight . . . and arrives in time.

A driving will, always.

In London, she falls ill, scarlet fever. For a month, an eon, she doesn't play. One night, a V-2 rocket lands a few blocks from her building, right in Hyde Park. Recovered, she manages to appear at the Royal Albert Hall. Then she is in Brussels, staying in the private apartments of Queen Elisabeth of Bavaria, and in Ostend, where, backstage, she meets Maurice Chevalier. His account: "Big impression, few violinists have ever touched me so deeply, in my most secret fibres. From the first notes, you are electrified by her genius. She seems possessed by a demon!"

The magnetic presence of Ginette Neveu is captured in a performance of Chausson's *Poème*, filmed in 1946 with the London Philharmonic Orchestra under the direction of Issay Alexandrovich Dobrowen. Chin held high, she takes a deep breath as though preparing to leap a hurdle. The bow slowly descends, lifts, while her fingers deliver a vibrato. Wearing a dress with puffy sleeves, Ginette rises at the centre of the stage, her arm falls.

+

1947. South America by train. Rio de Janeiro, Montevideo, Manaus, Patagonia, Bogotá. She meets André Maurois.

Then Mexico City, the United States—first Texas, Oklahoma, Utah—Canada, Carnegie Hall in New York City. On the flight home, at Christmastime, she improvises Ravel's *Tzigane* on the harmonica for the other passengers, her best concert, she would say. The aircraft circles over Orly Airport, impossible to land; the Constellation makes an emergency landing near Orléans, in a disused field that still carries marks of the war. To occupy the passengers, the captain organizes a game: "What would you do if you had a magic lamp and it could grant you one wish?" Some wish for wealth, renown, success, eternal life, Ginette hopes she can spend Christmas in her family's apartment on the square Delormel. A few hours later, her wish is granted.

+

On October 22, 1949, she goes with her mother to the rue Portalis, the Vatelot workshop. She is there to buy a Guadagnini, set aside for her by Marcel Vatelot, and to pick up her Stradivarius. From her intense playing style, the violin is subjected to excessive moisture, the young apprentice Étienne Vatelot, the luthier's son, has the job of opening the instrument slightly. A few weeks earlier, Étienne was chosen to accompany Ginette on her tour of the United States. She asks him to wait a bit before joining her. She plans, she says in her deep voice, to preview her programme in Saint Louis first, before starting the concert series she has lined up, and she won't be available before

November 10. Étienne has no reason to hurry and above all he doesn't want to be in the way, knowing that, in his line of work, discretion is key. He delays his departure, trades in his October 27 aeroplane ticket for a transatlantic crossing on an ocean liner.

17 *Bomber in a Cargo Plane*

> Plane accident kills boxer Marcel Cerdan. The press has
> thrown itself on his fresh corpse. "Get your photograph
> (20 francs) of the late Marcel Cerdan," special edition—
> what a deal...what vomit...And tomorrow, unashamed,
> I'll become a journalist again...because society gets the
> journalists it deserves.
>
> —René Fallet, *Carnets de jeunesse* (Youthful notebooks)

In Paris, the daily papers mine the Azores saga until
the seam peters out. After all the theories constructed,
experts questioned, and stories spun about the expedition, there is the wait for the solemn funeral rites. Delays
ensue, while the newspaper hacks fill their columns with
statistics: 585,851 persons have crossed the Atlantic since
1945, in 20,205 flights back and forth. During the week of
All Saints' Day, the daily gazette includes a catalogue of
forgotten names, overthrown ministries, news snippets,
anniversaries, and festivities. Front-page bulletins, news

under exclamatory headlines, vignetted ads, photo essays, special editions, an amalgam of collaged papers that offers up, to the cries of the hawkers on the street and the roar of the rotary press, the exquisite corpse of the unstoppable progress of the world. At top speed, miniaturized and spooled on strips of microfilm, the news flashes by. From fast-forward, to enlargement, to fine focus, the events cross paths and coalesce, while the noise of the machine awakens the dead. Nineteen Breton sailors die in a storm, and we still have no news of three fishing vessels — Metalworkers take to battle stations on orders from their union — Another match between France and Yugoslavia ends in a tie (1–1), drawing sixty thousand spectators to Colombes, where the game is played without incident — In politics, Georges Bidault finally fills his cabinet — The hole-in-the-ceiling gang sets off an alarm and flees empty-handed, leaving two suitcases behind with 130 lbs. of tools: prybars, cold chisels, fuses, knotted ropes, rubber slip-ons, a set of jacks, screwdrivers, not to mention...their handy umbrella, for catching rubble when drilling through the floors — Louis Armstrong wows the audience at the Salle Pleyel — Promotional insert: "I am a secretary, and I have a good job. I owe it all to the professional training I received at the PIGIER secretarial school." — A seaplane crashes in London: six deaths — The 63rd anniversary of the presentation of the Statue of Liberty, France's gift to the United States — Two young scientists set out for Chad, M. and Mme Jean-Paul Leboeuf sailed from Bordeaux this morning for West Africa aboard the steamer *Brazza*. Commissioned by the Musée de l'Homme and the National Centre for Scientific Research, they are travelling to the Chad region. They will take part in archaeological research to uncover the remains of ancient African civilizations — Book review: Maurice Nadeau on the subject of Robert Desnos: "He embodied the best aspect of surrealism: a furious hunger to achieve the impossible." An unpublished letter from H. G. Wells to James Joyce: "Your last two works have been more exciting and amusing to write than they will ever be to read." Who will be awarded the Prix Goncourt in 1949 — will it be Robert Merle for *Week-end à Zuydcoote* or Louis Guilloux for *Le Jeu de patience*? — Advertisement: "Now that they have a choice, customers are more demanding. For breakfast, they want a quality brand with a long-established reputation...they want BANANIA, the exquisite chocolate-flavoured breakfast beverage." — Arrest of the alleged Setty murderer, this evening the London police arrested Brain Donald Hume as an accomplice in the murder of automobile dealer Stanley Setty, whose torso, missing its head and legs, was found five days ago in a marsh in Essex — On the silver screen, Roberto Rossellini's *Stromboli*, with Ingrid Bergman, George Cukor's *Adam's Rib* (under the title *Madame porte la culotte*), with Katharine Hepburn and Spencer Tracy, and, in its eighth week of box-office success, *Retour à la vie* (*Return to Life*), with Bernard Blier, Louis Jouvet, and Serge Reggiani — It is a frigid All Saints' Day, and flowers are expensive, the traditional visits to cemeteries began two days ago. At the Paris flower market and at stalls next to cemetery gates, the price of flowers has risen 15 to 30 percent over last year. Vendors complain about the drop in sales, but even a meagre stem of chrysanthemums costs 200 francs.

+

In the Azores, the Day of the Dead, November 1, 1949, has never been more aptly named. Mass is being celebrated continuously on the island in honour of the Constellation's victims. The locals have begun to feel affection for the passengers, their mourning tinged with pride, the fleeting sense that, for a few days at least, they are at the epicentre of a global tragedy. They learn the names of the dead, Ginette Neveu, Marcel Cerdan, and wear mourning for the crash victims, who by the will of providence have become their own dead. It will take almost a week before the bodies are returned to France. The French consul, Morin, has arrived in São Miguel and now coordinates operations. The thirty-three French coffins wait at the Ponta Delgada barracks while the experts continue their investigations and establish the identity of each victim. On Monday, November 7, in the early afternoon, the grim cargo is loaded onto a vessel plying between São Miguel and Santa Maria, where airborne hearses await it on the landing strip, three LB-30 Liberator cargo planes provided by the International Air Transport Society (SATI). Huge, slab-sided aircraft, built in Detroit's assembly plants and destined for the British Allies, they fly according to the dictates of the commercial world. Fanned out across the tarmac, the identical triplets, their loading ramps deployed, will swallow—like the whale in Walt Disney's *Pinocchio*—the mortal remains of the Paris–New York flight. On Tuesday, November 8, at dawn, cargo aircraft F-ooAF takes on board the bodies of the thirty-three French nationals for a two-tier flight: a jink to Casablanca to drop off Cerdan, then a second leg to Cormeilles-en-Vexin, Orly's annex.

The trade winds at its back, the cargo plane flies over the Strait of Gibraltar, then begins its descent toward Casablanca and the Camp Cazes aerodrome. Is anyone aware that the Constellation's pilot, Jean de La Noüe, is returning to a land he knows well? A land that Bernard Boutet de Monvel painted? The throng crowding the runways mourns a boxer named after an aeroplane. At 10:00 a.m. local time, carried down the boarding ramp of a cargo Liberator on four shoulders, comes Cerdan, the Bomber. A continuous double line of grieving fans attends the coffin along the palm-fringed road to Lyautey Stadium. In the sports arena, at the end of the avenue d'Amade, in a hastily built hotbox of a chapel, thousands of Casablancans file past the catafalque where the champion will lie until his burial.

18 *The Reno Divorcés*

Don't ever tell anybody anything. If you do,
you start missing everybody.
—J. D. Salinger, *The Catcher in the Rye*

I had read, in a contemporary press cutting, an anecdote
about one of the passengers aboard the Constellation.
His name was Ernest Lowenstein, the owner of two tanneries, one in Strasbourg, the other in Casablanca. It said
he had divorced a month earlier in Reno and was going
to New York for the sole purpose of trying to reconcile
with his wife. The story struck me, I imagined the telegram sent a week before the plane flew, something like:
ARRIVING NEW YORK 28 OCTOBER STOP CONSTEL-
LATION F-BAZN STOP LET'S MEET STOP I MISS YOU
STOP. I was fascinated by the history of Reno, Nevada. The
city became the divorce capital of the United States at the
beginning of the twentieth century and continued in that
role until the late 1960s. A federal law had made divorce

proceedings easier, no proof of adultery was required, a claim of "incompatibility" or "mental cruelty" was enough to obtain the precious document. Wanting to kill two birds with one stone, the local authorities gradually decreased the residency requirement from six months to six weeks, making Reno a tourist town with a sideline in divorce. I learned that Mary Pickford, the silent film star, came to live there for six months in 1920 to speed her divorce from Owen Moore and fly into the arms of Douglas Fairbanks. There were also tales of the Riverside Hotel, the great stars of Hollywood staying there when they wanted to expedite their breakups, including Paulette Goddard coming in 1935 to end her marriage to Charlie Chaplin. I discovered an American popular song:

> I'm on my way to Reno,
> I'm leaving town today
> Give my regards to all the boys
> And girls along Broadway
> Once I get my liberty,
> No more wedding bells for me
> Shouting the battle cry of Freedom!

I pushed my research further, hoping to find more information about Ernest Lowenstein. Finally, on November 2, 2013, I came across an article that appeared on October 31, 1949, in the *Ironwood Daily Globe*, a Michigan newspaper. At the time, I was stupidly enjoying the paper's name, *Daily Globe*, it reminded me of the paper for which Peter Parker worked, the photographer-hero of the *Spider-Man* comics. An article entitled "The Hope That Failed" described the victims' families, waiting at New York's Idlewild Airport. It told how the rumour of possible survivors, debunked a few hours later, had encouraged a vain hope and exacerbated the despair of friends and family. The photograph accompanying the article captured the precise moment of that hope. The caption read: "Mrs. Ernest Lowenstein of New York hugs her nine-year-old son, Bobby, having heard from a friend that her ex-husband, Ernest Lowenstein, of New York and Casablanca, survived the Air France crash in the Azores. The rumour shortly proved to be false. There were no survivors. Mrs. Lowenstein said she had obtained a divorce in Reno a month ago, but that her husband was returning to the United States to discuss a reconciliation." Bobby, nine years old at the time of the crash, he should be traceable … Robert Lowenstein, born in 1940, there can't be tons of them, the child in the photo would be seventy-three now, there's a good chance he's still alive. Google turned up three possibilities, one of them a child psychiatrist in Pittsburgh, Robert Aaron Lowenstein. I found his e-mail address on the clinic's website and wrote him this message:

Date: November 2, 2013, 00:57:54
Topic: Ernest Lowenstein
Dear Doctor Lowenstein,
    My name is Adrien Bosc, I am working on the plane crash F-BAZN Constellation.

I'm not sure you're the son of Ernest Lowenstein, if so may I ask
you a few questions?

Best regards,

Adrien Bosc

Two hours later, I received a reply, which I read when
I awoke:

I am his son. What questions do you have?

Sent from my iPhone

I'd written on the off chance, and the truth is I didn't
think I'd find him so easily. When I reread my e-mail, I was
a little embarrassed. I'd begun my query abruptly and without any real precaution, not considering the strangeness of
my topic line, "Ernest Lowenstein", sixty-four years after
what had surely been the major tragedy of his son's life.
There was a vulture side to it, crassly journalistic, in fact.

After several exchanges, we agreed on a telephone conversation on Sunday, November 10. I explained my project
to him, told him that I wanted to hear his version and not
rely just on the press clippings. Reassured, he told me the
story of his parents:

*My father, Ernest, was a German Jew, who was born in
Westphalia and immigrated to Paris in the late 1930s. He
worked for my uncle in the leather business. My mother
was Polish and had also immigrated to France. They met*

in Paris. In 1940, when the Germans arrived, my father was away. He had enlisted in the Foreign Legion and was on a combat mission in Algeria. My mother, then pregnant with me, decided to leave Paris. She managed to cross the Pyrenees into Spain. A French family helped her by giving her a ride in their car. From Spain, she took a boat to Casablanca, where I was born. My father came from Algeria to join us. We spent the entire war in Morocco, with my father working first as a policeman, then starting a tannery. In 1945, we immigrated to the United States. My father's business took off after the war, and he travelled a great deal between New York, Morocco, and France, where he had started a second processing plant. We spoke French at home, it was my first language. We also spoke German and Polish. Then, in the summer of 1949, my parents divorced. I remember the trip to Reno, which seemed like a holiday. My mother and I lived there for six weeks. I didn't understand everything that was happening. It was summertime and it just seemed like a holiday. Then there was the Air France flight, they told us he had survived, and then they told us there were no survivors. A few days later, his body was identified. Lots of reporters staked out our house. The story of the reconciliation is true. I knew that was the point of his trip, and that my mother was favourable to the idea. She was a very energetic woman. After my father's death, she became one of the first female stockbrokers in New York. My mother was very enterprising.

I studied in Chicago, then at Columbia University. I became a psychiatrist, specializing in childhood and *adolescent trauma. I practised for a long time in New York City, then we moved to Pittsburgh.*

My father was a truly good man, very loving. What's funny is that he enjoyed sports, boxing especially. So you can imagine, for Marcel to be on the same plane... I'm still working at the age of seventy-three, I love my job.

[I ask him if he thinks there's any link between his work and the tragedy.]

Yes, of course, I've always wanted to help children overcome their traumas, my rapport with children comes from this event. And it was very strange to get your e-mail, coming out of nowhere...

I also want to say that we were very surprised at the time when Air France sent us some money by way of compensation. It was an absurdly small amount, I don't remember how much, but it was truly ridiculous.

[I speak of the lawsuit brought by the Hennessy family, which was thrown out of court on appeal.]

Oh yes, I remember that, I read about it in the papers. No, really, it was ridiculous.

I thanked him and hung up.

I thought about us, our memories. About the singer Emile Latimer, whom we saw in a Nina Simone concert video. From our shared pleasure in coincidences and our attraction to public figures who have faded away came the idea for a book that we would coauthor. We called the project *Red Circles*. We discussed several of the portraits—a degree candidate in a book by Pierre Sudreau, a photograph by Roy DeCarava of John Coltrane and Ben Webster, Jackson C. Frank and his song "Blues Run the Game". We talked about Ginette Neveu.

19 *Cormeilles-en-Vexin*

Chance looks like us.

— Georges Bernanos, *Sous le soleil de Satan* (*Under Satan's Sun*)

After the stop in Morocco, the Liberator cargo plane makes straight for Orly Airport's annex in Cormeilles-en-Vexin. Below the fuselage, the Moroccan coast scrolls past, Rabat, Kenitra, Tangiers, the Mediterranean basin with its outlet at Gibraltar, Málaga, Granada, Saragossa, the Pyrenees and their smugglers' trail, then Toulouse, Limoges, Orléans, nine hours on a colonial diagonal from one continent to another. Early evening and the Liberator, piloted by Roger Loubry, is making its approach. Clearance comes from the control tower to land on runway number four, not far from the SATI buildings. Once taxiing, the aeroplane is directed towards the company's hangars, far from the reporters clustered in the reception hall of the airport.

Behind closed doors, shielded from sight, the coffins are extracted one by one from the aircraft's rear and lined up side by side; outside, a fleet of hearses awaits them. Grouped by church, the thirty-three casualties are distributed among the convoys to Saint-Augustin, Père-Lachaise, Saint-Jean, and the provinces. Didier Daurat is there: a friend of Jean Mermoz, the aviator, and of Saint-Exupéry, immortalized as Rivière in the latter's *Night Flight* and now the director of Air France's operating centre. The undisputed master of the mails, Daurat recognized Saint-Exupéry's talent and named him dispatch manager on the Saharan coast. Valuing steadiness over stunt flying, he initially assigned Mermoz to cleaning engines, saying, "What I need are not circus performers but bus drivers. We'll train you." Right now, the bus he is looking at is a grisly one.

The final convoy of F-BAZN passengers sets out at 9:00 p.m., the hearses, accompanied by the national motorcycle police, cross the tarmac and roar towards Paris at breakneck speed.

+

At the exact same moment, on this night of November 8, 1949, and for the first time in Paris, the English singer Kathleen Ferrier gives a recital at the Salle Gaveau. The incomparable voice of "Klever Kaff" reverberates in the concert hall as though it were a requiem mass. Synchronic magic, two women prodigies, one a violinist, the other a contralto, joined by the coincidence of a date, communicating to each other *de profundis*. The simultaneous occurrence of these two events, joined by no causal link, the arrival of the mortal remains from Constellation F-BAZN in Paris and the recital by the British singer that same night at the same hour, forms one of the many pervasive *objective chances*, invisible to us until they are brought together, in many ways like those stars that twinkle in the night sky and are clumped into constellations by the eye and the mind. The numbered and linked points in a colouring book. A strained coincidence or the workings of fate, who is to say, and yet the game of temporal co-occurrences yields the most astonishing associations. In a famous case of Carl Jung's, a patient is in the act of describing a dream about a golden scarab when a scarab beetle bumps into the window—a june bug, opening the door to doubt.

Kathleen Ferrier and Ginette Neveu, two sisters in fate, two exceptional and truncated careers, two shooting stars. They had met two months earlier at the Edinburgh Festival, where they performed on the same stage. At the dinner afterwards, they were happy to note that they would both be touring the United States at the same time, and as they said good-bye they promised to see each other in New York no matter what. This plan was to remain a dead letter. Three days after the crash in the Azores, Kathleen Ferrier wrote to a friend in Wisconsin, Benita Cress:

London

October 31, 1949

My dear Benita,

There were two lovely letters waiting for me when I arrived home yesterday—I am so glad you are happy about the concert—my gosh I hope I don't let you down!

It will be lovely to stay with you—please can I go to bed in the afternoon?—just so's I don't talk too much, and clear mi old brain with a bit of sleep. I wonder how long it will take to get to New Mexico—Santa Fe—by train? I don't want to fly in January—I hate it any time. Have just been staggered by the death of Ginette Neveu in a plane crash to the USA—she was one of the finest fiddlers in the world and just 30! Just can't think why that should have had to happen—also her brother killed at the same time—isn't it a waste!...

Bless you, love, we're fine for everything—we've managed at last to get a 2nd-hand ice-box, so life's a lot easier, and our nylons will last until I get to America again—we don't have them here at all but I stocked up well last trip!

Kathleen

Ginette and Kathleen had a friend in common, the conductor John Barbirolli. Could he have imagined that he would survive them both and deliver both their funeral orations? "I count my joys," Kathleen Ferrier once wrote, and Barbirolli knew two of them, the greatest female musicians of the postwar era, brought together by the force of destiny, on November 8, 1949, in Paris.

20 *Holy Year*

And yet, O Lord, I have braved a perilous voyage
To stare at a beryl graven with your image.
— Blaise Cendrars, "Les Pâques à New York"
   ("Easter in New York")

Montreal, August 1949, Guy Jasmin and his mother sail on the *Empress of France*. It is the same boat on which Roger Lemelin arrived back in Canada a week earlier, wreathed in success for his novel *Au pied de la pente douce* (*The Town Below*), just published in France by Flammarion. The Pente-Douce, the working-class district in Montreal Guy likes to explore. Executive editor of *Le Canada*, devoted son and confirmed bachelor, he accepts an invitation from the French commissariat general for the lead-up to the Holy Year of 1950, wanting to make his mother's dream of visiting the Catholic pilgrimage sites come true. Guy Jasmin chose a career in journalism early in life, working for Olivar Asselin, his guide and mentor. During the 1930s in Montreal, he and his friend Willie Chevalier worked their way up the chain of command at the big Quebec newspapers. Before long, one of them was at *Le Canada*, and the other at *Le Soleil*. During World War II, Guy volunteered for an aid organization that helped French refugees. He discovered France through the stories of the expatriates. Someday, he would go there. In December 1948, he met a young Frenchman who taught at the Collège Stanislas, a certain Valéry Giscard d'Estaing. Guy told him of his upcoming trip in August, and they agreed to meet in Paris. In the summer of 1949, his reportage on preparations for the Holy Year would take him to Lisieux, Lourdes, Italy and the Vatican, and on a side trip to the Côte d'Azur. His mother had been a musician, and they planned to attend a performance of *Nabucco* at the Teatro dell'Opera in Rome and a big farewell concert that Ginette Neveu was giving at the Salle Pleyel in Paris just a week before their scheduled return to Canada.

What a surprise, on the night of October 27, to find the virtuoso standing beside them at the foot of the boarding ramp. Rachel can't get over it. She has kept the programme of the farewell concert and makes a point, once they are on the plane, of getting the violinist to sign it.

Guy had been impressed by his visit, and his articles reflected his enthusiasm. The Holy Year, he said at a Canadian embassy lunch the day before their departure, would leave its mark on the history of Christianity.

Guy's articles encouraged Quebec's Christians to sign up for trips organized by their parishes. Did any follow his recommendation? No one knows, but exactly a year later, on October 27, 1950, a group of Canadian pilgrims landed in Lisbon on the ocean liner *Columbia*. After a visit to the town of Fatima, they made a first stop in France at Lourdes, then went on to Paris and Lisieux. High point of the pilgrimage, an audience with Pope Pius XII at the Vatican on November 13. From there they went to Ciampino Airport, where they boarded a plane to go back to Paris. The aircraft, a DC-4 built by Curtiss-Reid, took off at 2:16 p.m. An hour later, the plane slammed into a mountain, the Grande Tête de l'Obiou in the Isère, on the heights above La Salette. There were no survivors. Rescuers reached the wreck the next day to discover the extent of the catastrophe. The most far-fetched theories were proposed to explain the accident, with some saying that the plane was downed by the Russians, anxious to recover secret Vatican documents travelling with the pilgrims to the United States.

Crocodiles don't follow funerals, as they can't cry.
— Francis Picabia

Orly, November 8, 1949 — The Air France company celebrates its two-thousandth transatlantic flight with great pomp. Champagne, caviar, and lobsters replace the regular aeroplane meals.

✝

Église Saint-Augustin, Paris, November 9, 1949 — The night before, the eleven coffins of the crew members of Constellation F-BAZN were placed in the crypt of the Church of Saint Augustine. Family, friends, unknowns, and officials from the company and various ministries gathered at 11:00 a.m. to pay their last respects to the aircrew fatalities. In the centre of the nave, under metal arches that support large wrought-iron flower shaped chandeliers, an honour guard of colleagues from the company extends on either side from the benches to the altar. Wearing uniforms that bear Air France's sea horse insignia, nicknamed "the shrimp", the company's flight personnel stand in ranks. The Église Saint-Augustin is a stigma at the heart of the capital, a big wedding cake of varied Byzantine inspiration, a mixture of white stone and metal arcades, an absurdity as inappropriate as Sacré-Coeur Basilica, that rude insult to the defeated ideals of the Paris Commune. Before the service, hundreds of curious Parisians walk in solemn ceremony as far as the coffins, an influx that stops only when the doors are shut. In the front rows, grieving families, ranks of gauze veils and dark suits; a few rows back, the officials, consequential ones, including Max Hymans, chief executive officer of Air France, representatives from the French cabinet, the Seine prefecture, the police, the air force, and, on the end, Inspector Lévis-Mirepoix, who ferried the dead souls from the Azores. The absolution of the dead is performed by Monsignor Leclerc, then the crowd disperses to the sustained notes of the grand organ. In the forecourt, the coffins of the aircrew are loaded into hearses and scattered to their places of burial: Jean de La Noüe, the captain, returns to his village on the Brittany coast, Pléneuf-Val-André.

Central office of the undertakers, 66 Boulevard Richard-Lenoir—The passengers of Constellation F-BAZN are laid out for their families. On each coffin, the name and official certificate of identity. The final identification of the bodies is to occur before they are transported to the cemeteries, soon they will return to family crypts—in the Basque country for the shepherds, in Alsace for Amélie Ringler and René Hauth, in L'Haÿ-les-Roses for Paul Genser, in Bagneux for Jo Longman, and in the Père-Lachaise Cemetery for Ginette Neveu and the six unidentifieds, who will be grouped together in a Tomb of the Unknown Passenger. It was built for the nameless bodies when, with their identities in doubt, the foreign nations to which they possibly belonged declined to repatriate them. Their number included, perhaps, Remigio Hernandores, Hanna Abbott, Yaccob Raffo, Eghline Askhan, Mustapha Abdouni, and James Zebiner, stateless persons in East Paris.

Saint-Laurent Cemetery, 805 Avenue Sainte-Croix, Montreal— The bodies of Guy and Rachel Jasmin arrive in Montreal on November 7, and, two days later, the Québécois journalist community congregates at the Church of Sainte-Madeleine d'Outremont to pay its respects to the editor in chief of *Le Canada* and his mother. Every newspaper in the country, even *Time* magazine from New York, has sent a representative. Guy's friend Arthur Prévost reads aloud a postcard that Guy wrote the day before the flight.

Church of Notre-Dame-de-Lourdes, Casablanca, November 10, 1949— Casablancans have been filing past the boxer's mortal remains continuously for two days. The crowd's pain-filled fever is a shadow image of its victory celebration. A long line snakes out into the tree-bordered alleyways of Lyautey Park. Under Morocco's dazzling autumn sun, devastated faces, sombre and stricken, wait patiently in hopes of a few moments of quiet recollection. Nightfall doesn't stop the procession of anonymous mourners, and the garlands and wreaths collect around the coffin, which is decorated with a capital "C" and surrounded by the ropes of a boxing ring. At regular intervals, the guards clear the room of its offerings. Ten guest registers have already filled with signatures. Casablanca has come to a halt, the funeral will last as long as it has to, the suffering is enormous.

At 10:00 a.m. on November 10, the champion's funeral service is held at the Church of Notre-Dame-de-Lourdes. It takes nearly fifty taxis to transport the accumulated heaps of flowers there. The motorcade to Anfa resembles a military parade. The weather is splendid, the day a special holiday, and seventy thousand people gather around the church building. Inside are the Moroccan royal family; the wife of Resident General Juin; M. Francis Lacoste, minister plenipotentiary; M. Négrier, director of the civil cabinet; M. Grémaux, president of the French Boxing Federation, who arrived that very morning at 4:00 a.m. In the front rows are the Cerdan family, Marinette and her three children, the cousins, uncles, friends. René Cerdan, the nephew, an apprentice boxer and Marcel's sparring partner this past summer, sprinkles holy water. Inconsolable, he collapses on the coffin. Former manager Lucien Roupp is also on hand. After the service, the procession winds around to Ben M'Sik cemetery. The priest delivers the funeral oration, and the gravediggers fill in the first shovelfuls of dirt.

+

Back in the central office of the undertakers, 66 Boulevard Richard-Lenoir—Ginette Neveu was to be buried on November 9 at the Père-Lachaise Cemetery. As to Jean, his body was never found. Her grave marker in section 11 was carved with a violin in bas-relief, and on the headstone was a bronze medallion with the profile of the violinist and this inscription:

ICI REPOSE

GINETTE NEVEU

1919–1949

À LA MÉMOIRE DE JEAN NEVEU

SON FRÈRE

1918–1949

TOUS DEUX VICTIMES

DE LA CATASTROPHE

AÉRIENNE DES AÇORES

LE 28 OCTOBRE 1949

HERE LIES

GINETTE NEVEU

1919–1949

TO THE MEMORY OF JEAN NEVEU
HER BROTHER
1918–1949
BOTH WERE VICTIMS
OF THE AIR DISASTER
IN THE AZORES
OCTOBER 28, 1949

And yet the burial was cancelled. At the headquarters of the undertakers, Marie-Jeanne Ronze-Neveu refused to identify her daughter's body.

Learn how to sell to buy to resell.
— Blaise Cendrars, "Tu es plus belle que le ciel et la mer"
   ("You Are More Beautiful Than the Sky and the Sea")

Aeroplane flight is a luxury. The only working-class passengers — the five Basque shepherds and Amélie Ringler, the spool operator from Mulhouse — were on board solely because the former had U.S. contracts and the latter's godmother had summoned her. "Aeroplane of the Stars", trumpet the Air France brochures, the travellers are privileged beings, an elite. It's also the means of transportation chosen by men in a hurry, businessmen. On the night of October 27, those boarding at Orly Airport are New World traders, import–export specialists. A Tower of Babel, the list printed in the newspapers further enlarges the spectrum of continents the passengers represent. A precipitate of the whole world, whose chemical formula might be unpacked as follows:

John Abbott, fifty-four, was returning from Syria with his wife, Hanna, thirty-four, whom he married a month earlier. They lived in Butte, Montana.

Mustapha Abdouni, twenty-seven, a Syrian-born farmer, on his way to meet his wife in Logan, Utah, where he was to see his twenty-one-month-old son for the first time.

Joseph Aharony, forty-five, an Israeli lawyer.

Eghline Askhan, thirty-four, a Turkish importer.

Edouard Gehring, twenty-nine, an American manufacturer.

Remigio Hernandores, forty-nine, a Cuban industrialist.

Emery Komios, thirty-two, an American lawyer.

Yaccob Raffo, twenty-three, an Iraqi chauffeur.

Maud Ryan, née Gibrat, fifty-three, had married an American soldier in 1919. She was returning from a visit to her French family. She lived in Atlantic City.

Margarida Sales, née Castel, thirty-nine; her husband, Philip Sales, forty, a New York exporter.

Raoul Sibernagel, fifty-nine, president of the Selsi Company of New York, an optical equipment importer, was returning from a business trip to Paris. His wife remained hopeful until the last possible moment, saying to reporters in the reception area at Idlewild airport: "If there are any survivors, my husband will be one of them, he has always been lucky!"

Irene Sivanich, fifty-seven, of Detroit, a widow and an emigrant from Yugoslavia. She had been visiting her mother.

Edward Supine, thirty-nine, a Brooklyn lace importer, was returning from a visit to the lace workshops in Calais.

James Zebiner, fifty-two, a Mexican businessman.

23 Red for Ginette, Green for Amélie

Twice have I, victorious, crossed the Acheron:
Playing in turn on Orpheus's lyre
The sighs of the Saint, the cries of the Enchantress.
— Gérard de Nerval, "El Desdichado"

The young woman's body at the funeral parlour, with its blackened face and green dress, is not her daughter, she is sure of it, she insists. The fingernails are much too long, Ginette's are trimmed short so that they won't interfere when she plays. The staff reason with Marie-Jeanne Ronze-Neveu, they even repeat the myth about hair and nails continuing to grow after death. The atmosphere is oppressive, the officials, sure of their ground, agree in low tones that the woman is suffering from denial. It is nothing of the sort. The dress does not belong to her daughter, the necklace with the Egyptian medallion is one she has never seen before, the body's slender build has nothing to do with her daughter's broad shoulders. Marie-Jeanne won't relent, grows excited, and the corpse is finally transferred to the coroner's office. After an examination of the teeth, there can be no doubt. It's not Ginette Neveu. They look through the unknowns, who will be buried together in the commemorative vault at Père-Lachaise within a few hours, for any sign of the young prodigy. Only one woman is discovered among the six mangled bodies, and it is patently not Ginette. To the family's grief over her death is added the torment of uncertainty. Fate is intent on punishing the Neveus, who learn that the body of neither child has returned from the Azores.

An error is possible, someone theorizes. Ginette's brother-in-law, M. Barret, leads the investigation. He examines the Air France passenger list, concentrates on the women between twenty and thirty, several names fit the bill: Amélie Ringler, the spooler from Mulhouse, twenty-seven; Hanna Abbott, Syrian, thirty-four; Françoise Brandière, French-Cuban law student, twenty-one; Thérèse Etchepare, Basque shepherdess, twenty-one; Suzanne Roig, stewardess, thirty. Armed with a clue, the Egyptian medal, he calls each of the families. On November 26, he manages to reach Xavier Ringler, Amélie's father. It is unquestionably his daughter's pendant, and, in tears, the man announces that his daughter was buried on November 11 at the cemetery in Bantzenheim. After calling the prefecture of the Haut-Rhin department, Barret goes immediately to Mulhouse, where he visits the Ringler family, 24 passage Marignan. They describe the funeral, he is led to the grave. At 8:00 a.m., the employees of the undertakers dig up the zinc coffin and open it with a pry bar. No question, the red dress with beige sleeves belongs to Barret's sister-in-law Ginette. A hearse carries the coffin back to Paris. On November 29, the Neveu family assembles at the Père-Lachaise Cemetery, section 11, a few plots from Frédéric Chopin, and Ginette Neveu is finally laid to rest. At the same time, Xavier Ringler travels to Paris to identify Amélie's body; within a few days, a funeral is again held in Bantzenheim. A new grave is dug, the right one this time. The other will remain empty. Only a wooden cross planted in twice-disturbed soil indicates the mishap of the red dress and the green.

24 *Prosopopoeia*

Written kisses don't reach their destination,
ghosts drink them along the way.

— Franz Kafka, *Letters to Milena*

The results of the investigation failed to provide an explanation for the tragedy in the Azores. The metal viscera of
the carcass revealed nothing of the Constellation's secret.
How did the plane drift to the neighbouring island of São
Miguel, and what concatenation of circumstances led to its
colliding with the mountain's peak? What devil contrived
to coordinate so many errors, causing a crash whose prob-
ability was nearly zero?

This *nearly* at the centre of attention, this chance element whose consequences must be teased out to separate
it from pure fate. Two laws govern the history of flight and
combine in the public mind to transform a chain of ratio-
nal causes into a magical sign of fate: the law of series and
Murphy's law. The first comes from a blindness towards

happy outcomes and the stress put by the media on tragic events within a series. The second, its corollary, derives from the absurd notion that a succession of mishaps proves a catastrophe to be predestined: "Everything that can go wrong, will go wrong." The worst-case-scenario concept has governed the rules of aviation, which tries to beat the odds by resorting to precaution. In 1949, there was still no way to make the dead speak. The ancestor of the black box, the hussenograph, an audioless photographic recorder invented by François Hussenot, is not yet in general use. All the investigators have to go on are the radio exchanges with ground control and the plane's wreckage. Once these two leads have been exhausted, an exact reenactment of the flight might possibly bring the relevant errors to light. The shadow aircraft, a Lockheed Constellation, registration F-BAZO, will retrace the flight path and attempt to initiate a dialogue from beyond the grave with the wading bird of the Azores. In rhetorical terms, the aeroplane preparing to take off from Orly on December 7, 1949, is a prosopopoeia. This book is not one. The fiction of an omniscient narrator, slipping into the victims' clothes as you might change costumes in a small theatre of the period, is not proposed. The description of the flight, the arrangement of the characters within the whole as represented by the plane is the only viewpoint, the only theatricality. Let's hope it doesn't hide any others. The crew of the shadow aircraft was appointed by a ministerial order, published in the *Journal officiel* for November 9, 1949. It includes Lévis-Mirepoix, the inspector for civil and commercial aviation, and Fournier, the air force's chief operating engineer. Also in the crew were Maurice Bellonte, head of Air France's accident investigation division; Jean Dabry, who will man the controls, a pilot of similar experience to F-BAZN's captain, Jean de La Noüe; several navigators; and an engineer from the French Weather Bureau. Representatives of the manufacturer, Lockheed Aircraft, concerned for the fate of the Constellation, are also present. The witness-plane takes off from the runway at Orly at 4:00 p.m.

At the weigh-in, F-BAZO and F-BAZN box in the same division — middleweight. On my right, Constellation F-BAZO, weighing 62,644 pounds. It was awarded its airworthiness certificate on February 27, 1948, and went into service on March 21, flying the seventy-seven-hour run from Paris to Saigon via Cairo, Karachi, and Calcutta. Five years after it joined the long-distance transport fleet to the Southeast Asian colonies, Indochina would gain its independence. On my left, Constellation F-BAZN, weighing 61,365 pounds, airworthiness certificate dated February 26, 1947, damaged on April 6, 1949, during a rough landing on the tarmac at Orly, de-icing port wingtip section, wing damaged along six and a half feet, far rear panel of the port upper wing surface creased over eight inches and breached over one inch at right angles to the end rib and the aileron hinge. Other than these details, the two aeroplanes are identical, F-BAZO fills its role as a sparring partner perfectly and is ready to shadowbox, or rather shadowfly, along the southern route to the Americas for the investigating commission's report. The ghostly recapitulation will deviate from the path of the October 27 flight, however, making two stops along the way, the first in Madrid to take on representatives of the Spanish air force, and the second in Lisbon, where the director of Portuguese civil aviation and the liaison official for airlines will board.

+

Making the dead speak, turning tables and summoning spirits back for a last curtain call, asking a voice to encore from the beyond. The survivors are gangrened, gnawed at by absence. An army of inconsolables, imploring the mute graves for a sign, awakened in the night by a call that is only absence, tattooing its presence. Édith Piaf sinks into the realm of the dead, she is convinced that she will find the boxer again. "I am sure that Marcel is alive and waiting for me," she says. The crash has become an obsession, the black mark of her fate: "It's the first time I've fallen in love, and, whoosh, it's all whisked away. They break my heart, tear him from me. Leave him smashed up. I'd like to die, but I worry that I won't find him again if I commit suicide," she writes to her friend, the actor Robert Dalban. The fear of dying and not finding him again. In early December, she gets a call from Marie-Jeanne Ronze-Neveu. A long conversation that Édith draws out as much as possible. Finally a sister in grief who understands her, hears her. Ginette's mother says she talked with her daughter late one night.

She experienced great joy from it, was reassured to find her daughter at peace. The account makes Édith hopeful, but also jealous — why is she unable to talk with Marcel? She becomes a religious zealot, haunts churches, buys a rosary, visits a synagogue, calls on sorcerers, fortune-tellers, charlatans of every stripe. Then, at an antiques dealer's in America, she finds a pedestal table, the thing she has most wanted, a bridge to the other world. Michel Emer, her friend and the composer of the song "L'Accordéoniste", tells her of the spiritual séances Victor Hugo held on the island of Guernsey. Nocturnal calls to Hauteville House, the turning table a link to his departed daughter Léopoldine. A three-legged pedestal table that rapped out up to four thousand words at a time. And the spirits that streamed into the poet's drawing room — Chateaubriand, Dante, Aeschylus, Rousseau, Machiavelli, André Chénier, who came to put the final touches on an unfinished sonnet, Shakespeare, who dictated a new tragedy, *The Dank Forest*. The table, or, as Victor Hugo called it, "the shadow's mouth", urged him to keep writing, "the novel belongs to tomorrow", it rapped out with its wooden tongue. Édith is hoping to hear Marcel forgive her, she knows she is at fault, she telephoned for him to come, she made him change his ticket, take the October 27 flight, she believes she robbed him of his life to indulge a whim. She herself had a phobia about aeroplanes, and when her friends would try to reassure her before a flight, saying that her hour had not yet come, she would retort, "And what if the pilot's hour has come?" Why had she, selfish and impatient, overridden this fear, she asked herself? After many table-turning sessions, Marcel comes back. He talks to her, reassures her. After a brief reunion, the magic table moves on, reproaches Édith for stinginess. The table starts giving financial advice, essentially to promote the interests of her close friend Momone. The spirit-world contact turns blackmailer, Édith stops trusting it, turns away. She won't again encourage the dead to speak.

According to legend, "Hymne à l'amour" was written in response to Marcel Cerdan's death. This is false. The song was written in the spring of 1949 and was first intended for Yvette Giraud, a young singer whom Édith had taken under her wing. Her 1959 song "La Belle histoire d'amour" would be her hymn to Cerdan: "It's your voice that I hear / Your eyes that I see / Your hand that I look for / I belong only to you."

Four years before her death, writing her autobiography, *Au bal de la chance* (*The Wheel of Fortune*), Piaf said, "I'd have travelled a thousand miles to hear the great Ginette Neveu."

25 Final News From Alsace

"You know where they'll send me. Beyond the Maginot Line:
it's a guaranteed death trap."
— Jean-Paul Sartre, *The Age of Reason*

René Hauth willingly gave up his post as managing editor
of the daily newspaper *Dernières nouvelles d'Alsace*. Assigned
to French Army headquarters, he joined the counterespio-
nage division, which was posted to the Luxembourg front in
January 1940. The offices of BREM, the Regional Bureau for
Military Studies, had been installed in Longeville-lès-Metz.
The group was deployed to forward posts along the Maginot Line and kept tabs on German espionage on the other
side of the border. Whole nights, alternating with his aco-
lyte Auguste Clément, trying to record coded transmissions,
drafting report after report, and cross-checking contradictory information to determine the date, hour, and place of
the invasion and forestall a surprise offensive. In early April,
with the blessing of the government of Luxembourg, he

helped install a warning system to supplement the existing telephone network in the event of an attack. A giant set of shortwave transmitters and receivers placed along the Luxembourg border. René, a militant pacifist and a former journalist for *Le Progrès civique*, had believed in the "war to end all wars", he'd pilloried war profiteers and argued for strengthening the League of Nations. He identified as a radical socialist and worked, according to the weekly's mission statement, to create "an honest paper for honest people". Now, the idea of world peace, mediated by dialogue and conciliation, seemed a thousand miles away. He feared the return of trench warfare, doubted the generals' defence strategy, the myth of the impregnable Maginot Line, a fairy tale for the doughboys, thought this man who was eavesdropping on the Wehrmacht's preparations. The attack would be massive, nothing like the bayonet ranks facing off across the Chemin des Dames, the tanks would crush the antiquated resistance and impose the law of the lightning bolt.

At 4:30 a.m. on May 10, 1940, the German Army crosses the border into Luxembourg, and, as expected, the warning system helps make up for the disabled telephone network. Close at hand, René follows the advance of the enemy's troops and the retreat of the Allied regiments. In the afternoon, the priority shifts from organizing a defence to helping part of the population cross into France along with Luxembourg's government and its royal family. With Lieutenant Doudot, he coordinates the removal of barricades from across the road between Rodange and Longwy to help the general exodus. Then he is assigned a mission of the highest importance — to ensure the safety and extraction from Luxembourg of Grand Duchess Charlotte. Top secret, eyes only. He counted it a high feat of arms, this backward "Flight to Varennes", this counterrevolution of outmoded dignitaries who, after barely twenty-four hours, packed their bags and fled. His orders were to accompany the convoy as far as Longwy-Haut, where Captain Archen would take over and lead the royal family to the Château de Montastruc in the Dordogne.

The Phoney War was under way, René volunteered for a mission in the Balkans. Nothing is known of this journey. As a good spy, he asked his wife, Marguerite, to burn every scrap of documentary evidence before his departure. The French Army signed an armistice on June 17, marking the end of his mission as a double agent. In early July, he arranged to meet his wife and brother in Lyon and told them he was leaving for the United States, where he would try to enlist with the Free French Forces. His family would stay in Alsace, in his brother's keeping. For five years he tried by every possible means to join the Allied intelligence services: being from Alsace proved an obstacle. And so, he lived a double life. He haunted the waiting rooms of officialdom, settled, bought a house, and finally managed to contribute to the American espionage services — deciphering code, translating, radio jamming, low-level tasks far from the secrets of Enigma.

On May 8, 1945, the war over, René took the first available ship to France. His one thought was to convince his wife to immigrate to the United States while he found work as a foreign correspondent for *Combat* or *l'Aurore*. The conversation went nowhere, out of the question, she had been waiting five years for him, he would abandon his dream of America immediately and resume his place as managing editor of *Dernières nouvelles d'Alsace*, at 17 rue de la Nuée-Bleue. In October 1949, resigned to life in Alsace, he decides to sell the house in New York. A last few details require his presence there. On October 27, aboard Air France's F-BAZN, René Hauth puts an end to his American dream.

In November, an Air France employee calls the Hauth residence. René's widow answers, they explain the situation to her: the body of her husband has not been identified, does she want him buried in a communal crypt at Père-Lachaise or does she want an empty coffin sent back to Alsace? Her brother-in-law is listening to the conversation. It's out of the question for René to be one of the dead with no grave. His cousin René Fontaine, a medical school professor, would be able to identify Hauth and offers to visit the mortuary on boulevard Richard-Lenoir, accompanied by the dead man's dentist. They identify his body within minutes — without the benefit of science, searching the pockets of one of the anonymous corpses, they find René's passport. No wedding ring. Had he been robbed of it by looters on the mountainside? Horrible rumours were circulating, stories of fingers being chopped off. On their return, Marguerite reassures them. René often played golf, and as the ring bothered him, they had an agreement that she would wear both.

26 Symphony for Solo Plane

> Machines create such a large number and variety of noises
> that pure sound, because of its weakness and monotony,
> no longer elicits any emotion.
> — Luigi Russolo, *The Art of Noise*

On October 5, 1949, the first work by Pierre Schaeffer, *Five Studies of Noises*, is broadcast on French television. A "concert of noises" comprising five pieces: "Disconcerting, or Study with Automatic Sprinklers"; "Imposed, or Study with Railroad"; "Concertante, or Study for Orchestra"; "Composed, or Piano Study"; "Pathétique, or Study with Pots." Together with Pierre Henry, Schaeffer founds the Group for Concrete Music Research, and together they record the two-record *Symphony for Solo Man*. Two parts of the work bear the title "Prosopopoeia". Their research focuses on arranging noises, composing with concrete elements derived from the real world that, laid end to end, will form a continuous sound, music. In December 1949, at the very

moment when Constellation F-BAZO is in the air mim-
icking the tragic flight of Air France's F-BAZN to try to
uncover some of the factors, Pierre Schaeffer formalizes
his art of noise in the journal *Polyphonie*, calling it "concrete music". In this manifesto on animate sound, he writes:
"This practice of composing with elements sampled from
available experimental sounds I intentionally name 'Concrete Music', to signal our dependence, not on preconceived
abstract sounds, but on sound fragments that exist con-
cretely, taken as definite and integral sound objects." You
might say, What relation does this have to the story of the
aeroplane downed in the Azores and the re-creation of its
flight by Air France's investigative unit? I answer, Not much
really, except a certain kinship and, looking back and noting
strange correspondences, the synchronicity of certain dates.
In line with Pierre Schaeffer's "Study with Railroad" — a
recording of steam locomotives — the section of the flight
re-created by F-BAZO during the night of December 7 to 8,
1949, could have been called "Study with Flight Plan". The
French aviation inspectors travelling in the Constellation's
chromed tube are looking for sounds — discordant, continuous, or absent — they track noise and the breakdown of
noise, they are radiophonic technicians. You doubt this, you
find the comparison overblown, yet the job of these men is
to strain to hear, huddled in an airframe over the Atlantic,
the radio-electric guidance mechanisms strung in a line,
like Tom Thumb's pebbles, as beacons along the southern
route to America. To hear this aeronautical music, you need

to know your music theory. The flight of the investigating commission will give us a fine opportunity to practise our scales. Its primary mission is to ensure, as it flies the exact route of the downed aircraft, the good working order of the navigational signals and radio beacons all along the line between Orly and Santa Maria. A radio beacon, as its name suggests, broadcasts from a known location, allowing a ship or aircraft to calculate its position relative to the beacon on the earth's surface, using a radio-electric guidance system known as a "sonic road". A series of radio beacons can be used to trace lines on a chart whose intersection marks the receiver's exact location.

The paths thus traced virtually in the sky compose a sonar signal linked by long distances to the transmitting beacons on the ground. Their carrying range depends on weather conditions—during a storm, for instance, the signal is weaker. How does this sound map manifest itself inside the plane? It's fairly simple: if the aircraft drifts to the right of the traced route, the radio operator hears a series of long sounds, called "dashes"; if it drifts to the left, he hears a series of short sounds, called "dots"; and, of course, when the pilot keeps the plane flying within the airway determined by the transmitters on the ground, the dots and dashes meld to form an uninterrupted tone. In the case of Constellation F-BAZN, the fact that it crashed into Mount Redondo testifies that it drifted considerably off course. Why did the flight deviate north in the archipelago, and why was the crew not warned by the control tower at Santa Maria during the landing protocol a few minutes before impact? This is what the civil aviation inspectors are going to try to find out during the simulation.

After stopping in Madrid and Lisbon, Jean Dabry, the pilot of Constellation F-BAZO, heads for the archipelago and, at the Azores intersection, picks up the fatal route taken by his predecessor.

27 The Forty-Ninth Victim of the Constellation

Each loss, each passing of a beloved singer or artist,
ineluctably became an occasion for national mourning.
— Stefan Zweig, *The World of Yesterday*

The first time Margarête Froehmel heard Ginette Neveu's playing at an international competition in Vienna in 1931, it was a revelation. She was moved to tears by this girl of twelve, whose Bach Chaconne stood out from her competitors', most of them adults. Since then, Margarête had not missed one of the virtuoso's tours through Austria, and she methodically clipped any news accounts of her in the papers. Her big scrapbook contained articles about the Wieniawski Competition prize in March 1935, Ginette's concerts in Germany, and her tours to the Soviet Union and the United States. A matted photograph of Ginette decorated the leather cover of the scrapbook, which was as meticulously bound as the books Margarête looked after in the municipal library for Vienna's ninth borough. She was the library director. Her husband had died on the Russian front, conscripted into the Wehrmacht two years after the Anschluss. The library had been partially destroyed during the siege of Vienna in April 1945. The arrival of the Red Army on April 13 marked the end of Nazi occupation. The capital was just a field of ruins, and the sight of Russian soldiers filing in for three whole days had traumatized the population.

The Vienna Philharmonic had been terribly affected by the war. As early as 1935, the pervasive anti-Semitism was contaminating even the arts. Three days before the premiere of Richard Strauss's *The Silent Woman*, Stefan Zweig's name was removed from the publicity posters as the libretto's author. In 1938, Wilhelm Jerger, a member of the SS, was named head of the Philharmonic. Nazification decimated the orchestra's roster of musicians, six Jewish musicians were killed, and ten others were deported to the death camps.

Margarête carefully collected Ginette's EMI recordings, the Brahms and Sibelius concertos, Debussy's Sonata, Ravel's *Tzigane*, Suk's *Four Pieces for Violin and Piano*, and the opus 25 *Poème* by Chausson. The vinyl records played in constant rotation on her phonograph, until the microgrooves of her 78 rpm's were worn. Margarête's fascination shaded into obsession. Hearing that Ginette Neveu intended to play a series of concerts, she rushed to the Philharmonic to be sure of getting a ticket for every performance. Transported for seven evenings by the violinist's Stradivarius, she was fortunate enough on leaving the last recital to meet her, talk to her. She felt it was the start of a friendship, Ginette had given her her Paris address, they could write back and forth.

On the evening of October 31, 1949, Margarête starts to read that day's *Die Presse*. On page four, she finds an article about the distant tragedy in the Azores. She takes down the photograph of Ginette Neveu, cuts the page from the newspaper, and writes in pencil along the bottom, "*Ich bin verzweifelt...*" (I am in despair). She goes to the kitchen, takes the hose from the gas heater, clamps her teeth around it, and pushes the button. She is discovered on November 1, stretched out, clutching the photograph and the article. Newspapers around the world carry the story. To the casualty list was added the name of the woman henceforth known as "the forty-ninth victim of the Constellation".

Don't get stuck in the ruts of the results.

—René Char, *Feuillets d'Hypnos* (*Leaves of Hypnos*)

Off Lisbon, the flight crew of F-BAZO, the shadow plane, starts keeping a record of its manual radio compass readings. Everything is scrupulously noted—reception of radio beacons in the area, interference from the ground transmitter in Portugal, exchanges with the control tower in the Azores. By the end of the investigation, they will have to understand the reasons for the deviation of Constellation F-BAZN—almost fifty-five miles from its intended position. An analysis of the aeroplane's wreckage has already exonerated the manufacturer. The flight re-creation is an attempt to explore the only plausible trail remaining, namely conditions on the approach to the archipelago. Without a black box, piloting errors can't be verified. It is therefore crucial for the experts to analyse the flight's every detail between Lisbon and Santa Maria.

Over the Atlantic, a few hundred miles from Portugal, a first and still minor incident comes to the attention of the investigating commission. The aircraft is unable to receive signal BB7 from Santana Airport. There is interference between two signals: the radio beacon from the Azores, which the navigators are unable to receive, and the signal from Seville, Spain, which, though hundreds of miles away, they receive perfectly, five out of five. The detail is important. At this stage in the flight, the opposite should be occurring, and the distant signal from land should be growing fainter as they draw away. The anomaly persists for the remainder of the flight. At 9:53 p.m., Seville is still at five out of five, the signal only weakening slightly at 10:22 p.m. The crossing of the radio waves throws the plane off course, sending it several dozen miles to the north, just as happened to the fatal flight on October 27. When the signal from São Miguel finally comes in at a strength of two out of five, an hour and a half before arrival time, it suddenly disappears off the radar for seven minutes, at the very moment when the Air France inspectors are flying over Algarvia Peak, the site of the crash... Faulty functioning of the radio beacon due to interference from the Seville transmitter now seems the likeliest cause of the accident. The pilot's last words, "I have the field in sight!" remain a mystery. What airfield was he looking at? At that moment, a few seconds before crashing, how could he have seen anything that looked like a landing strip with runway lights?

The weather conditions on São Miguel on the night of October 27, unlike those on Santa Maria Island, were particularly bad. Approaching the archipelago, the pilots, as we remember, were surprised at not finding the clear skies described by the control tower at Santa Maria a few minutes earlier. The pilot, bringing the plane in for a landing after traversing a dense layer of clouds, must have been fooled by the refracted lights of the village of Provoação at the foot of the mountain, only recently wired for electricity. The neighbouring glow would have been something like an aurora borealis. The weather was heavy, the pilot, led into error by the reduced visibility, took the nimbus of light scattered in the summit area for a landing strip. There was a vanishing chance that the aircraft's altitude would correspond with the height of the summit — another few dozen metres and the Constellation would have sailed clear. "God does not play dice," the saying goes, but on the night of October 27 to 28, Constellation F-BAZN scored a Yahtzee.

On July 26, 1950, the investigating commission delivers its report to the Transportation Ministry. Here are its conclusions:

> *While unable to exclude entirely the possibility of a map-reading error, the commission believes that BAZN's faulty navigation was due to the sudden failure at the end of the flight, unsuspected*

*by the crew, of certain aspects of its radio direction finding
reception, either an abnormal propagation of radio waves or
the faulty functioning of its equipment. This cause was exacerbated by overconfidence, resulting from favourable atmospheric
conditions in the arrival zone, conditions that led the captain
not to verify his radio bearings as he would have done in worse
weather. A visual confusion in the darkness was a final result.*

Constellation F-BAZO fulfilled its mission, rejoined Air
France's Paris–Saigon circuit. Coincidence of dates, again
and always, it was sold in 1971 to the Macon Estate and
junked on a certain October 27.

29 *Hennessy v. Air France*

For us, there was life, true life, real life, no matter how bad
it had seemed, before the accident, and nothing that came
after the accident resembled it in any important way.
— Russell Banks, *The Sweet Hereafter*

Walk along the Hudson, in autumn, dead leaves carpet the
walkway, the splotches of red and orange make for slippery
footing; reflected, the winter sun shatters, fine slivers at
the edges of your eyesight, you lower your head, hands in
the pockets of a heavy coat, belted at the waist, a naked
tree planted on the promenade; in spring, the shells on the
water, their rhythms alternating, recede on lengthening
wakes; its lawn invaded, the riverbank becomes a recre-
ational boat basin, and in the sweltering heat of an American summer the children dash into the water while the
community looks on. Simone Hennessy has taken the habit
of setting off alone every Sunday on a blazed walk from Liv-
ingston Manor to Waterfront Park, a peaceful prairie carved

out vertically above the Hudson River. Two hours stolen from her schedule, two hours she has negotiated, leaving her daughters, Eileen and Bridget, with their father, to go for a little spin, as she liked to say. At the farthest point, the railway station, where the weekday ritual of scurrying white-collar workers — their newspaper tucked under one arm, leaving behind suburbia, their wives and children, for New York City, its offices and secretaries — gave way to an urban desert, there she would sit, on the same bench in front of the railway platform. She scribbled in a little note-book, always in French, not to-do lists, but stray thoughts, seasonal haikus, her journal, which she never reread, confined to a present made of general truths. They had moved to the United States twelve years ago, leaving behind Old Europe and their two big families, the Hennessys and the Broches, brought happily together through them. Patrick started his architectural firm in Manhattan, and they spent the prewar years in Washington Square, migrating after the birth of their eldest, Bridget, to Dobbs Ferry, in West-chester County, an entirely respectable suburb an hour by train from the business district. An important site during the American Revolution as an encampment for General Washington's army, Dobbs Ferry now had a following among bankers and advertising executives. When the war ended, Patrick embarked on a series of profitable real estate ventures, snapping up old neo-Gothic residences that had once belonged to aristocrats and turning them into luxury apartments. His last coup was the purchase of 155 Beacon

Hill Drive, a sumptuous late-nineteenth-century mansion straight out of *The Magnificent Ambersons*, whose interior might easily hold entwined staircases harbouring in their shadowy recesses the concealed face of George Minafer. Patrick kept its exterior intact, subdivided the space inside, and called the whole thing "Castle Apartments".

The marriage was floundering, the two children and Simone were homesick for France, she dreamed of returning there one day and visited more and more often, a month in August 1946 with Bridget and Eileen, three weeks at Christmas in 1947. She never warmed to the bleak life of a suburban mother. A cohort of neurotic women, cheated on, zealously religious, imprisoned in a rosy picture of success. Friendships that were not really friendships, meaningless conversations, phony conviviality, boredom of the kind that latches on to you and won't let go, crass habits, and all *joie de vivre* put on the shelf. In January 1949, husband and wife were separated. In October, she goes to Paris to settle her father's estate, her two daughters stay in Dobbs Ferry, the nanny, Eileen Sheridan, looks after them. Simone prepares their return to France, rents an apartment in the 6th Arrondissement, and sets off to fetch her daughters on October 27 by the Air France flight.

Patrick Hennessy learns of Simone's death on October 28, all doubt is gone, there are no survivors. He rushes to his daughters' sides, uncertain how to console them, he has never known, so he holds them in his arms and does what he can to dry their tears. Eight and ten years old. They fall asleep from exhaustion, poleaxed. On October 29, he decides to take the first flight for Paris, to wait there for the body of his ex-wife, to identify her at the morgue, to attend to all the formalities. The girls will be in the care of their nanny, they will join him in a week. In December, he starts legal proceedings, a battle that will last almost five years. He sues Air France for 25 million francs ($71,000) in compensation, rather than accept the 2,200,000 francs ($6,300) set by international law. Divorced, he says he is fighting on his children's behalf. His lawyer, Marcel Héraud, blames the pilot and the fact that the navigational instruments weren't thoroughly checked. The court finds in Air France's favour on two occasions, and, on February 3, 1954, Patrick Hennessy drops his suit. The case becomes a textbook example, cited as *Hennessy v. Air France*.

Confused wailings, litanies, whispers, which the sceptical
or distracted may easily mistake for the noise of
the sea or the crying of vultures. Many are the souls
of shipwrecked sailors.

—Antonio Tabucchi, *The Woman of Porto Pim*

Going to the island finally became inevitable. Following the
procession, backward, towards the crest of the mountain,
looking for the remains of the aircraft, most likely buried
under thick layers of ferns.

On the morning of October 28, a boat belonging to
the Atlânticoline company sets out for Ponta Delgada from
Vila do Porto. Sixty-four years earlier, as the sun rose over
the archipelago, small boats were still scanning the ocean
for parts of the downed aeroplane, and search planes were
flying low over the area.

On the bridge, the sense of taking part in a mimetic pilgrimage, no doubt grotesque, driven by a maniacal concern

with synchrony, to the point of making my itinerary coincide with the dates of the expedition. So it's at noon, approaching Ponta Delgada, that I join the first crew alerted by the search plane. No one is waiting for me, unless it's the bus travelling the shoreline of São Miguel Island that, turning at the foot of the mountain, heads for the village of Povoação. I have reserved a room in a bed-and-breakfast, facing the ocean. The next day, at noon, I will proceed to Algarvia and, with Lévis-Mirepoix's expedition, begin the ascent of Mount Redondo, while a fine rain falls, a sort of liquid mist, an atomizer's halo. After hours of hiking through the forest, following paths blazed with paint marks, the mountain's crest appears, and it is only after following the ridgeline to the end of a narrow, exposed trail that the famous shadow of the Redondo nipple appears, where the last remains of the Constellation, overgrown with time and native grasses, lie. The only marker is a stone erected by the inhabitants of the village in honour of the forty-eight victims of Air France's F-BAZN, a commemorative edifice known by the name *alminhas*, "little souls". A granite cross, the base tiled in ceramic squares, with a blue-painted text describing the site:

LOCAL ONDE CAIU NO DIA
27 DE OUTUBRO DE 1949
UM AVIÀO DE AIR FRANCE
TENDO MORRIDO TODA
A SUA TRIPULAÇÀO
E OS PASSAGEIROS.

DAI-LHES SENHOR
O ETERNO DESCANSO...

PLACE WHERE FELL
ON OCTOBER 27, 1949,
AN AIR FRANCE AEROPLANE
CAUSING THE DEATH OF ALL
ITS CREW MEMBERS
AND ITS PASSENGERS.
GIVE THEM, LORD,
ETERNAL REST...

Two sets of initials appear at the top of the marker, "PN" and "AM", *Pater Noster* and *Ave Maria*. I searched through the dense foliage for a few rusty bits of the mechanical skeleton, a riveted sacred shroud, relics of my pilgrimage. The last pieces of the aircraft lie several feet below the surface, under the carpet of mosses, eaten away by their decades-old destruction. The bulk of the carcass, junked in the weeks following the crash, found a second life God only knows where on São Miguel.

The archipelago is constellated with *almas* or *alminhas*, "souls" or "little souls", cubes of stone with blue and white tiles, topped by a cross. According to local legend, the souls circle the stones on November 2, hoping that Saint Michael will catch them with his rope and fish them out of Purgatory. The crosses, of which there are a great many on the heights of São Miguel, watch over the rescue of those shipwrecked at sea. On the summit of Mount Redondo, a soul watches over the salvation of forty-eight people shipwrecked in the sky.

+

My last day in the archipelago, I went to look at whales, beyond the folded hills on which the island's peasant farmers graze their bleating ewes. At Lajes do Pico, the Captain Ahabs with their shallow nets, the emigrants washed onto the dock from the ocean crossroads, and the farmers who had swapped their pitchforks for makeshift harpoons have all been replaced by excursion boats that ply Pico's waters on a fixed schedule, for tour operators who guarantee a glimpse of whales or your money back. Offshore, far from the coastline, the whale's silvery blue skin, striped with lines of lighter blue, emerges from the water, ferrying ultrasonic songs up from the deep. I'd like to tell you about Antonio Tabucchi and *The Woman of Porto Pim*, a collection of tales set in the Azores. In the prologue, the Italian novelist warns you that the whales and shipwrecked sailors in his stories are symbols of the infinite and the absolute. On the bridge, my heart knotted by solitude and absence, I imagine the crash, the aeroplane and its passengers like transposed images of chance and coincidence. Every story is a pretext. These last two years, I have believed more than is reasonable in signs, in lucky stars, I have lost myself in them, only the story of these lives fatefully enclosed in the fuselage of a Constellation could answer my questions. I had needed to travel to the Azores to hear the intimate resonance of these men and women, who once lived and loved. I had had to reach Ponta Delgada, walk along the trails of Mount Redondo, watch late and early the sky and the shoreline, to see the illusion of distance at the heart of this novel. To understand that by getting away from the morass of my emotions I would in the end come up against a familiar landscape, find answers, put one foot in front of another again. One has always to set off, one's heart in a jumble, in search of whales. And in Pico, I might add, there are no lighthouses.

In Horta, on the island of Faial, there is a bar where sailors from all over the world congregate and leave messages, telegrams, bits of paper pinned to a wooden notice board that extends around the counter. This place, a waiting room for sailors of the Atlantic, an improvised post office, is called Peter's Bar. Legend has it that *Casablanca* was filmed here, that Louis Armstrong sang "As Time Goes By" at the back of the room. I believe it. The words affixed to the board await their addressees, urgency is beside the point, they will find takers or become dead letters. I remember a family story. My uncle, who was called up to serve in Algeria, and my father, a student in Paris, corresponded all through the war. The sole message contained in their letters was the position of the pieces in a chess game that they played by correspondence over the course of two years. I don't know who won, and I don't really care. Peter's Bar stands out at night in Horta like a beacon, and you sit there and get hammered until you see the sun at the bottom of your glass. You drink down your sorrows, you share those of your neighbour, you repair friendships dinged by a long crossing. In this refuge, each shipwrecked soul seeks out, and finds, the memory of his sorrow, and drinks beyond reason the wages of his regrets. While there, I drank down the bullrings of Granada, a lost garden in the middle of the Alhambra, a canopy bed with a wooden screen in Albayzín, and the Moorish fountain that sang a lullaby to soothe two wounded children. And, with the last glass, the Autobus bar near the Cirque d'Hiver in Paris, the mezzanine of the Café de la Mairie on the place Saint-Sulpice, and La Féline on the hill at Ménilmontant. I left, tacked to the bulletin board, between two bottles in the sea, this scrawled message torn from a notebook: "Someday we will tear down our prison walls; we will speak to people who answer; misunderstanding will vanish from among the living; the dead will have no secrets from us. Someday we will board trains that leave the station."

31 *The Guadagnini Scroll*

Grammarians are to authors what a violin maker
is to a musician.

—Voltaire, *Pensées, remarques et observations*
(*Thoughts, Remarks, and Observations*)

Étienne Vatelot started as an apprentice at the family workshop in 1942 at the age of seventeen. The young violin
maker gave up a career as a football goalie with no regrets.
At 11a rue Portalis, behind the Church of Saint Augustine,
an atmosphere of silence reigns, of humility, of secrets
shared in coded words, to the sole cadence of creaking
wood. On the tables covered in green baize, sick violins are
surrounded by wood screws, hand clamps, varnish brushes.
An inheritance not left by any will. A sixth sense, a feel, the
soul is heir to an intimate understanding of artist and instrument that no school can teach. You learn by methodically
repeating the same actions on practice violins: removing
the strings, tuning pegs, bridge, soul post, end pin, tailpiece,

nut, and fingerboard, tirelessly fieldstripping and reassembling your gun. Prying off the soundboard with a knife, removing the bass bar, the blocks, and scratching at drops of glue with a gouge. Lined up on the green cloth like an inventory: back, bridge, button, chin rest, corner block, end blocks, fingerboard, frog, heel, mortise, neck, nut, purfling, ribs and lining, scroll, shoulder rest, soul post, soundboard, thumb cushion, tuning pegs. A grammar, in preparation for handling the instrument, to which will eventually be added, as with writers, liberation from the constraints of syntax, through style. The sorcerer's apprentice scrutinizes the mystery and dreams, gouge in hand, of animating violins the way the brooms in *Fantasia* are made to dance.

It is a commonplace to write that a violin maker is a doctor to musicians. No violinist will deny the analogy, as the relationship between artisan and instrumentalist often extends far beyond the violin. The luthier can in some sense be a psychotherapist, a doctor of the soul, a comparison written into the very manufacture of the instrument. The soul post, the sprucewood dowel placed inside the resonating chamber. A few millimetres from the right foot of the bridge and the tailpiece, the soul post, also called the *âme*, after the French word for soul, just like the one found in each of us, if we care to believe in it, responds to our indefinable need for echo. It transmits the vibration of the strings to the instrument's back. It also allows the top plate to withstand the pressure exerted by the strings against the bridge. The *âme*, an echo chamber that withstands pressure, the weight of life, I can subscribe to that definition readily enough. A doctor of the soul, without a stethoscope but armed with as poetic a tool: a soul post setter. The luthier's art rests in significant part on the placement of this cylinder of wood. The artisan, in the process, becomes a confidant. The sound post must be adjusted to correspond to the personality, the very sonority, of the virtuoso. With his setting tool, the luthier spears the soul post and introduces it through the right f-hole, nudging it delicately into the correct position. Misplacing it by even a few millimetres can throw off the violin and the violinist's playing, handling the soul post of a violin requires a complete understanding of the instrument and its owner. And the *âme*'s doctor then becomes a doctor of souls. Étienne understood this when he accompanied his father to Austria to meet the sailors of the forests, the woodcutters of those sylvan cathedrals. Designing a violin for Menuhin, finding a tree fraternal in temperament to the virtuoso to make a soundboard in harmony with him. And from this voyage, the first in a long series, he retained the impression of belonging to an order of sorcerers, who gather in the shadow of evergreens to invoke the moon, the sap, the angle of the sun, and the moisture in the understory.

Étienne Vatelot meets Ginette Neveu in June 1949, a relationship of trust and friendship immediately springs up. He is given a few small tasks to perform on the Stradivarius. He must pry it open slightly and adjust the violin's humidity, which the virtuoso's intense playing drastically affects.

The keepers of her flame even say that after a concert, in a state of exaltation, her chin would bleed. Étienne inspects the instrument, tells his father he would like to replace the base bar, which he believes too old and short. The sorcerer's apprentice wants to chop the brooms with a hatchet, but Marcel Vatelot, the master, sends him back to his desk: "You, little violin maker, *you* want to alter a violin of this calibre? Remember that you must never destroy a sound when it corresponds to the player!" Étienne remembers the lesson, a deep understanding of the instrument can come only from faithful companionship with the artist. First exercise, he will accompany Ginette on her tour to the United States, standing next to her he will hear the subtleties. As her duty companion, he prepares to escort her with his first-aid kit. It will fall to him to look after her Omobono Stradivarius. The tickets have been bought, Étienne will fly on the Air France flight of October 27. But on October 22, when Ginette stops by the workshop to pick up her violin, she asks Étienne to put off his departure, just until she has previewed her programme in Saint Louis. In a panic, the young violin maker calls his brother, an employee with French Lines, a maritime transport company, who manages to find him a cabin on the ocean liner *Île de France*. His departure is set for October 30. When he learns of the crash of Constellation F-BAZN, on the morning of October 28, he can't help but think, despite his deep sadness, of his aborted departure and the discreet power of chance.

Thirty-three years later, on Wednesday, June 30, 1982, at 10:30 p.m., live on Antenne 2 television from studio 15 at the Buttes-Chaumont, Jacques Chancel devotes a broadcast of his show, *Le Grand Échiquier* (The great chessboard), to Étienne Vatelot. The episode is called "The âme or soul of the violin." The violin maker is joined by his friends and clients Isaac Stern and Mstislav Rostropovich. A few days before the show airs, Chancel receives a letter from the pianist Bernard Ringeissen: "I have a priceless gift for you, one that you can present live on television." After talking to him on the telephone, Jacques Chancel invites him to join the broadcast. In the second half of the show, the host asks Étienne Vatelot to talk about the violinist Ginette Neveu.

✛

JACQUES CHANCEL: This touches you directly, since you were originally meant to be on that aeroplane.

ÉTIENNE VATELOT: Yes, of course, it gives me a pang whenever I think of her, but I think of her because she was a very, very great violinist, and above all a woman whose temperament was very deep, broad, and open. It's strange because when Ginette Neveu had this accident, and when the plane had this accident in the Azores, they brought back to us in the workshop the case in which she kept her two violins, there was nothing left inside, not even a tiny bit of wood except for a bow, which was broken, and another bow with a signature that we immediately recognized. They asked us, "Do you know this bow?" — Yes, yes, of course. It's a bow inlaid with gold and tortoiseshell, signed "Hill & Sons" of London, an English violin maker. And I said to him, "But where did you find this bow?" — Coming back down the mountain after our search of the wreckage, we heard a man scraping away at a violin in a peasant hut. We went in, saw him holding this object, gold and tortoiseshell, and we asked him, "Is this yours?" and he answered, "No, no, I found it." At that point, my colleagues and I asked him, "But what about the violin he was holding?" and this person, this member of the Air France commission, said, "Oh, you know, it looked so old!" So we've never known exactly whether Ginette Neveu's violin survived or not.

JACQUES CHANCEL: Étienne Vatelot, I haven't told you, I didn't announce his name to the press, but we'll see whether that exchange was true or false. A pianist, who is not here as a pianist tonight — but we'll soon see him on *Le Grand Échiquier* — I didn't tell you he was here, a pianist has had something at home, an object that may relate to Ginette Neveu's violin. I'm talking about Bernard Ringeissen. You know this, you know that a pianist named Bernard Ringeissen has . . . He's here, I'm going to ask him to show what he has. I apologize for doing this to you on live television, but here he is. [*To Bernard Ringeissen*] Come and sit down.

ÉTIENNE VATELOT: You know, for years I've been hearing that you own something that belonged to Ginette Neveu, something that was found.

BERNARD RINGEISSEN: Yes, the French consul who had the unhappy task of seeing to all the formalities—the French consul who was in Lisbon at the time of the disaster and went to the Azores—found on the day following the crash in the hands of a fisherman a violin scroll. I was touring in Brazil, and when he showed me the scroll—I knew Ginette Neveu well—I was obviously very moved. He said to me, "Here, I'm going to give it to you." [*He reaches into the left pocket of his jacket.*] And here it is. [*He hands the scroll to Étienne Vatelot, the luthier examines it briefly, his voice grows hoarse, a heavy sigh, Isaac Stern puts his hand on his shoulder.*]

ÉTIENNE VATELOT: It's the head of the Guadagnini of Ginette Neveu! She had two violins, she had two violins in her case, it's the head of the Guadagnini of Ginette Neveu. [*As he speaks, the camera closes in on the luthier's trembling right hand, which holds the headstock.*] I recognize it right away, for me it's as though it were yesterday. [*Long silence.*] It's incredible, I apologize. [*He wipes away a tear.*] I don't even need my glasses to see it, generally I put my glasses on, but this is so astonishing. It's the violin, the last violin my father sold her before she left for the United States. It's absolutely true! A whole story is bound up in this.

JACQUES CHANCEL: How does it happen that the two of you never met?

ÉTIENNE VATELOT: I don't know, there was a confluence of events, at one point I heard about this, I also called a friend to get your address, and then, I don't know, you were...

BERNARD RINGEISSEN: It's a relic, it was a relic, you know, I didn't...I was so moved. At any rate, we are finding it again today, and I think I'll give it to the Conservatory.

[*THE SCROLL IS PASSED FROM HAND TO HAND.*]

ÉTIENNE VATELOT: So, it's definitely not the Stradivarius, it's the Guadagnini.

BERNARD RINGEISSEN: And what happened to the Stradivarius?

ÉTIENNE VATELOT: I still don't know.

JACQUES CHANCEL: Bernard Ringeissen, thank you, we'll have you back here soon.

[*ÉTIENNE VATELOT RETURNS THE SCROLL TO BERNARD RINGEISSEN, HOLDING BOTH OF HIS HANDS.*]

ÉTIENNE VATELOT: You keep it carefully.

JACQUES CHANCEL: I apologize for doing it this way, it wasn't to create an emotional moment, it was just so you two would have a chance to meet.

BERNARD RINGEISSEN: It was a moment of true emotion, and I think that came through.

ÉTIENNE VATELOT: Absolutely. It's better to think about something else, although the memory stays with you, a good memory.

ISAAC STERN: I have to say that I was so moved and touched by what happened here.

JACQUES CHANCEL: I saw you cry, Isaac Stern.

ISAAC STERN: I attended the last concert she gave before she died, it was the day she left on the aeroplane and met her death; I was at the concert, it was at the Châtelet, with her brother, a suite of sonatas, she played marvellously well, such a solid, an enormous understanding of the music, a truly glorious soul. And I was so touched to see what happened this evening. I should tell you that the Hayden we played was a little in memory of Ginette, because she truly counted for something in music. We don't have many people like her, it's very rare.

ⴰ

I came across this video clip by chance, late one night, and the scene left me dumbfounded. The tears in Étienne

Vatelot's voice, Isaac Stern's eyes, the delicacy and awk
wardness of Bernard Ringeissen, and Jacques Chancel, the
master of ceremonies, almost embarrassed by the surprise
he has engineered. I had to watch it a second time, attend
to the details, the palm of the violin maker's hand, the little piece of wood carved in Baroque volutes and whose
magical reappearance in front of the television cameras
after thirty-three years made the moment seem like a surrealist sketch. An image comes to mind, the scroll-woman,
a renewed version of Man Ray's *Le Violon d'Ingres*, where
the muse Kiki of Montparnasse, slightly in profile, with a
violin's f-holes overlaid on her back, becomes a woman-
instrument. Her knotted turban corresponds to the scroll,
known as the "head", whose aesthetic coils swathe the violin in its secret. The owner of this snapshot was none other
than André Breton, perhaps seeing it as one of the *objective
chances* that he collected, as you might inventory butter-
flies under glass. *Objective chance*, this lovely phrase, which
he theorized as being due to the interaction of personal
experiences of synchronicity. In *The Communicating Vessels*,
he deepens the notion of necessary chance: "Causality can
be understood only in connection with the category of
objective chance, one of the forms necessity manifests."
A practical work on apparitions, *Nadja* is interspersed with
photographs by Man Ray. The last of these had a deep effect
on me at the time, a view of the Palace of the Popes in Avignon from the island of La Barthelasse. On the left side is
a panel, LES AUBES (the dawns), part of a signboard for the

island's restaurant, Sous les Aubes (under the dawns). This photograph does not appear in the first edition of the book and is not by Man Ray. The photograph is by a friend, Valentine Hugo, wife of Jean Hugo, great-grandson of the poet who wrote "Demain, dès l'aube" ("Tomorrow, at Dawn"). A few years earlier, she had offered her husband a small pen-and-wash drawing by his famous ancestor, a horizon line entitled *Aube* (Dawn), André Breton and Jacqueline Lamba later gave their daughter this hopeful name. This last photograph in *Nadja*, taken on the banks of the Rhône, comes a few pages before the end of the book. André Breton ends the tale with a transcribed newspaper article:

> *X . . . , December 26. — The operator manning the wireless telegraph station on Sable Island captured a message fragment transmitted on Sunday night at such and such a time by the . . . The message said essentially, "Something is wrong," but it gave no indication of the plane's position at the time, and due to the extreme weather conditions and consequent interference, the operator was unable to understand anything more or engage in further communication.*
>
> *The message was transmitted on a wavelength of 625 metres; given the strength of the signal, the operator believed the plane to be within a radius of 80 kilometres, or 50 miles, of Sable Island.*

The magic scroll seems like the kind of artefact that you find in fairy tales as the object of a quest. It emerged from the beyond, this fragment of carved wood, bearing a message that has to be deciphered. And now, the *Tale of the Guadagnini Scroll*, where the head of a violin passes from hand to hand, from the Azores, to Brazil, to a television studio at the Buttes-Chaumont in Paris, on a broadcast called *Le Grand Échiquier*, to be identified by the last violin maker to have varnished the instrument thirty-three years earlier. Varnish, ultimate secret, apothecary's concoction, which Marcel Vatelot prepared in private on Sundays, away from prying eyes, according to a recipe that he gave his son only on his deathbed. Antonio Stradivari, for his part, took his varnish formula to the grave.

That leaves a mystery. What happened to Ginette Neveu's famous Stradivarius, a violin made in 1730 by Omobono Stradivari, son of the Cremona master? That old violin in the hands of an Azorean fisherman, and which the investigators, blinded by the gold and tortoiseshell of the bow, thought was unnecessary to recover, so "old" did it seem, was it Ginette Neveu's famous Stradivarius? Lévis-Mirepoix, the Air France inspector, had ingenuously told the Vatelots, "Oh, you know, it looked so old!" As the days passed, the mystery surrounding the famous violin deepened. Because of the instrument's exorbitant price, it seemed unthinkable not to look into it. The insurance company did just that. Three days later, two experts, accompanied by an interpreter, went to São Miguel Island, to the village of Algarvia, to look for the lost violin. The investigators followed

Lévis-Mirepoix's directions, questioned the fisherman. He claimed he didn't remember, that he had never owned a violin like that. After searching the village from top to bottom, combing the slopes of Mount Redondo, the experts went away empty-handed. The mystery turned into a legend. In the Azores, the old people tell the story that, in the 1950s, a madman went around scraping at the strings of a violin. It's the hamlet's secret, they embroider the story constantly, add details, he disappeared, he sold the instrument, which ended up in the United States, a rich trader bought it for a heap of gold. No one really knows.

On November 6, 2013, at the Hôtel Drouot, Paris, the consignment company Artemisia puts up for auction Marcel Cerdan's suitcase, found on the slopes of the mountain. The sale excites a small circle of specialist collectors. The rectangular suitcase of cream-coloured leather, worn and threadbare but intact, bears the initials "E.C." under a crown, representing, by the catalogue's account, a symbol of the love between Cerdan and Piaf. They supposedly discovered the suitcase in a secondhand store, one day when they were wandering in New York, and were surprised to find the singer's first name and the boxer's last together, which they hoped someday to unite. A scuffed label from the Cunard White Star shipping line was plastered to the back of the suitcase, a memento of a transatlantic crossing in 1946. On the fiftieth anniversary of Édith Piaf's death, the media made much of this story, tagging it "the suitcase of love". Bidding was expected to ramp up quickly above the estimate of five thousand to ten thousand euros. Only the reporter for *L'Équipe* noticed that the dates were wrong, the two lovers met in 1946 but didn't start their idyll until January 1948, the crossing never happened. It's a fake. The investigative report reveals the hoax on the morning of the sale, the suitcase finds no taker.

I'd made a note, on the plane that carried me to Lisbon, of a passage from a poem by Blaise Cendrars, "Fernando de Noronha":

> *From afar it appears a cathedral sunk of old*
> *Up close*
> *The island's colours are so intense that its green grass is gold*

I found this a faithful description of the Azores, the thrusting upward of volcanic rocks, thousand-year-old stalagmites whose quirky shapes form the reefs' architecture. And this green, which is everywhere, flamboyant, the soil fertile with lava and the landscapes stamped with motifs from Douanier Rousseau, virgin forests and a setting sun. Yet the Azores in no way resemble the Brazilian archipelago of Fernando de Noronha, where the tropical green drops to the turquoise blue of the lagoons. Twenty-one islands, scattered more than three hundred miles from Recife. In the investigation report of the Paris–Rio crash, a surprising link surfaced. Aircraft AF447 took off from Antônio Carlos Jobim Airport in Rio de Janeiro on the evening of May 31, 2009. At 2:14 a.m. on June 1, the plane disappeared off the radar. The Brazilian authorities organized an immediate search, but the first bodies were not pulled from the water until five days later. The aircraft, lying on the ocean floor at a depth of twelve thousand feet, could not be found. The first human remains were repatriated from the airport at Fernando de Noronha. The unknown crash site and the depth of the ocean slowed search efforts. Only in April 2011 was AF447 found. On May 16, the precious black boxes were recovered. The bodies were transported to the island for DNA and dental-record identification, 12 crew members and 216 passengers, including Silvio Barbato, conductor of the Brazilian Symphony Orchestra in Rio. On June 16, the vessel *Île de Sein*, responsible for body recovery in the Atlantic, landed at the port of Bayonne carrying 104 French victims, who were later transferred to the Institut Médico-Légal in Paris.

On September 28, 1915, during the French offensive in Champagne, Corporal Blaise Cendrars loses his right arm. During a feverish night of writing on September 1, 1916, he recovers his inspiration, a text that will become *The End of the World Filmed by the Angel of Notre Dame*. Under the sign of the constellation Orion, the phantom limb ascends to the sky, where, as his muse, it inspires him with the elastic verse of modern times, and the poet of the left hand is born. Orion, the blind giant, betrayed by Oenopion, is guided eastward by the child Cedalion on his shoulders in search of the sun's rays, which the oracle has said would heal him. His death from the sting of Artemis's scorpion raises him to the heavens. Scorpio and Orion side by side as constellations. Blaise transposes onto the Greek myth the personal myth of his sidereal hand. Torn from him, cast into the muddy morass of the paths of glory, it joins the nebulae of Orion like the five fingers of the hand. Enchantment, assumption of a writing hand that joins with Betelgeuse, the major star of the astral theme sparkles.

> *All during the war, I saw Orion over the parapet*
> *When the Zeppelins came to bombard Paris they always*
>   *came from Orion*
> *Today it is overhead*
> *The mainmast pierces the palm of this hand, hurting it*
> *The way my sliced-off hand hurts me, pierced by a contin-*
>   *ual sting*

Cendrars becomes the hermit of Aix-en-Province, where he lives quietly from 1940 on. His children are at the front, his lover, Raymone, in Brazil with Louis Jouvet's theatre troupe. The poet has stopped writing, he kills time in country inns, curses the Krauts from bars along the Cours Mirabeau, scours the shelves of the Méjanes Library, and, in a large apartment on the rue Clémenceau, watches over

"Mamanternelle," the eighty-four-year-old mother of his forever lover. Three years of silence, three years before the demon of writing, drowned by France's defeat, again dictates its law to him, the text will become *The Astonished Man*. Others follow, he writes about the Last Judgment, about the patron saint of aviation, Saint Joseph of Cupertino, an ace at levitation. Raymone has come home. Nearby, Laurin, another one-armed man, sabotages German trains; farther off in Céreste, René Char, another poet, aka Captain Alexandre, takes to the hills with the maquis. Following the Liberation, in October 1945, a young reporter by the name of Robert Doisneau photographs Blaise under an arbour in the garden, behind the cactuses and tall grasses, in shirtsleeves, a beret planted on his head and a cigarette screwed into the corner of his mouth. He is no longer the dandy in shabby clothes painted by Modigliani, but a grandfather, back from a thousand battles, wiser, living in exile, his creased face enlivened by half-shut eyes. At his worktable, the typewriter on one side, the glass and rum bottle on the other. Blaise ages, and the young come running. They visit Aix as if performing a pilgrimage. It tickles him.

Hard on the heels of Robert Doisneau comes René Fallet, just demobilized: "Monsieur Cendrars, you are fifty-six, I am eighteen, and you could be, as they say, my father, but I recognize you, celebrate you, love you ..." he writes. Not a father but a brother, a friendly hand to join in scouring bistro counters, breaking glasses at the Deux

Garçons, talking poetry, chameleons, birds, lilies, betting your life on a coin toss—someone to team up with. Words of sweet friendship. A disciple without discipline. The hermit of Saint-Victoire levies an army of lads with a wave of his friendly hand.

A young man, another, his son not by adoption but by blood, the pilot Rémy Sauser, dies while flying beyond the Mediterranean in Morocco. A dull pain, stunning, "a punch in the face," Blaise says to a friend. He finishes *The Bloody Hand*, writes by way of epigraph: "FOR MY SONS ODILON AND RÉMY WHEN THEY RETURN FROM WAR AND CAPTIVITY AND FOR THEIR SONS WHEN THOSE SONS TURN TWENTY ALAS!..." then adds a new paragraph as a postscript, as if it were a last message, telegraphing his pain:

Alas!... On November 26, 1945, a cable from Meknes (Morocco) informs me that Rémy was killed in an aeroplane accident. Poor Rémy, so happy to be flying over the Atlas Mountains every morning, so happy to be alive since returning from captivity in Krautland. It's too sad... But one of the privileges of this dangerous calling of fighter pilot is that you can be killed in mid-flight and die young. My son rests, among his similarly fallen comrades, in the small and already overpopulated square of sand in the Meknes cemetery reserved for airmen, each folded into his parachute, like mummies or larvae, waiting among the infidels, poor kids, for the sun of resurrection.

And Raymone, separated, found again, mourns Rémy as her son, her favourite. Once more acting in the theatre in Paris, she writes to Blaise: "I was sure I would never see Rémy again. When he kissed me, at the metro, he felt that my eyes were saying farewell, and he came back and clasped my hands..." The phantom limb syndrome of the amputee, the son forever linked to the body, hallucinosis, a pathology of the stump, Rémy comes back to haunt his father in a "last little postcard", sent on November 4, 1945: "Dear Blaise, My work is getting more and more interesting, and I'm delighted. Everything is great, my work, the weather, the grub (dates, oranges, and tangerines) and I hope to stay here until Easter, return to France in spring. I hope that everything is OK on your side too. Kisses. Rémy."

A monoplane lost in the Atlas Mountains of Morocco.

A Lockheed Constellation vaporized in the middle of the Atlantic.

+

When you love, you come back. A life of breaking the compass, opening up to the cardinal points, and then, at the far end of the world, discovering the commonplace. When you love, you come back. A life of playing hide-and-seek, cheating boredom, cheating death, and, at the far threshold, the old cabin, the origin, the treasure. When you love, you come back. Reviled, despairing, in a jumble, the mind gaudy with strange animals and utopian landscapes, to discover in the depths of the primeval forest a patient, protective sister soul. When you love, you come back. A life that leaves you breathless, Russia, eastern China, Panamanian uncles, the Amazon, whales off Tierra del Fuego, Amsterdam, Antwerp, the horizon declining at the equator, war and ships, a whole life under the sign of departure. Of arrival, an unexpected, a banal arrival, from right next door, and the *Odyssey* as a great detour. When you love, you come back. On October 27, 1949, at Sigriswil, in the Bernese Oberland, while a plane bearing the name Constellation takes off from Orly, the poet Blaise Cendrars marries the woman he has loved forever, Raymone Duchateau. The marriage of old lovers in a Swiss–German inn, first the engagement trip, the ring seals his return to his country of birth. Blaise, the stateless one, has found a state. Having left never to return, he finds in the village of Sigriswil, at the threshold of his life, the land of his ancestors. And he, a Swiss in flight afraid of never arriving who, when finally Raymone agrees to marry, finds his Ithaca in the faces of the peasants from the Oberland. In its history, its expressions, its noses, he recognizes intangible signs of his ancestry. In the genealogy of the winemakers of Lake Thun, a shared character, a brotherhood of the untamed, the rebelled. In the drawing room of the inn, partying with friends after the wedding, Blaise announces that he is writing a *Conquest of Sigriswil*. Nothing will come of it. In the small ninth-century church, looking at a painting on wood, he recognizes his forebears among the thirty solid bourgeois on the altarpiece; on October 27, 1949, at the moment when the Constellation is taking off at Orly, the separated but inseparable lovers join, the poet with the missing hand arrives at safe haven.

In 1956, Blaise Cendrars publishes his last novel, *Take Me to the End of the World!* The title is a call in counterfeit form, no exoticism, no fantasized travel account, but a man's truth. The end of the world, as a planet makes its revolution, is not far off. From the *threshold*, an initial, limiting value, the foot of a doorway marked by stone or wood, or else a term from the vocabulary of aviation, *displaced threshold*, near the beginning and end of a runway. He gives his testament, while the fantastic, the dream element in the shape of an endpoint, is here in Paris: "The end of the world is the Père-Lachaise cemetery."

On the ground floor of the apartment on the rue José-Maria-de-Heredia, Blaise Cendrars dies. Paralysed, he lives through an endless, month-long agony. On January 21, 1961, Raymone closes her husband's eyelids, Miriam holds her father's hand. Don't smile through your tears.

+

I was born on January 20, and at the age of eleven I questioned the date of my birth. I had found a birth announcement that my parents sent out, which gave the date as January 21. I asked them, but neither was able to give me a clear answer, the birth certificate and the family record differed. I was furious, couldn't understand why they waffled over the facts. I didn't know the date of my birth and had no definite astrological sign, January 20 being in Capricorn and January 21 in Aquarius. A matter of constellations. The answer would eventually come from the hospital. The records said January 20.

+

My thanks to Manuel Carcassonne, Bernard Chambaz, Benoît Heimermann, and Luc Widmaier.

My gratitude to Philippe Castellano, author of the invaluable articles "Il y a 60 ans: le Constellation de Marcel Cerdan disparaissait aux Açores", *Avions,* Nos. 173 and 174; to Dominique Grimault and Patrick Mahé, authors of *Piaf-Cerdan, un hymne à l'amour 1946–1949* (Paris: Robert Laffont, 2007); to Jacques Chancel, orchestrator of the miracle.